Santa
Claus in
Baghdad

and Other Stories about
Teens in the Arab World

Santa Claus in Baghdad

and Other Stories about Teens in the Arab World

ELSA MARSTON

INDIANA UNIVERSITY PRESS
Bloomington and Indianapolis

This book is a publication of

Indiana University Press
601 North Morton Street
Bloomington, IN 47404-3797 USA

http://iupress.indiana.edu

Telephone orders   800-842-6796
Fax orders   812-855-7931
Orders by e-mail   iuporder@indiana.edu

Chapters 1, 2, 3, 5, and 8 previously published in 2005 by George Braziller, Inc. as *Figs and Fate: Stories about Growing Up in the Arab World Today.* © 2005 by Elsa Marston. "The Olive Grove," previously published in *Soul Searching: Thirteen Stories about Faith and Belief,* edited by Lisa Rowe Fraustino, Simon & Schuster, 2002. © 2002 by Elsa Marston. "Scenes in a Roman Theater," previously published in *Memories of Sun: Stories of Africa and America,* edited by Jane Kurtz, Greenwillow, 2004. © 2004 by Elsa Marston.

The paper used in this publication meets the minimum requirements of American National Standard for Information Sciences—Permanence of Paper for Printed Library Materials, ANSI Z39.48-1984.

Manufactured in the United States of America

Library of Congress Cataloging-in-Publication Data

Marston, Elsa.
Santa Claus in Baghdad and other stories about teens in the Arab world / Elsa Marston.
    v.   cm.
A collection of eight stories, most previously published in other anthologies, about what it is like to grow up in the Middle East today. Includes notes which place the stories in context.
Contents: Santa Claus in Baghdad: a story from Iraq (2000) — Faces: a story from Syria — The hand of Fatima: a story from Lebanon — The olive grove: a story from Palestine — In line: a story from Egypt — Scenes in a Roman theater: a story from Tunisia — Honor: a story from Jordan — The plan: a story from a Palestinian refugee camp in Lebanon.
ISBN 978-0-253-22004-2 (pbk : alk. paper) 1. Middle East—Social life and customs—Juvenile fiction. 2. Arab countries—Social life and customs—Juvenile fiction. [1. Middle East—Social life and customs—Fiction. 2. Arab countries—Social life and customs—Fiction. 3. Conduct of life—Fiction. 4. Coming of age—Fiction 5. Short stories.] I. Title.
PZ7.M356755San 2008
[Fic]—dc22

                                                    2007050768

3   4   5   13   12   11   10   09

For the young people of the Middle East
. . . may they grow in health and happiness, and con-
tribute to a more peaceful future.

And with my love, for Iliya,
who never lost hope that this could happen.

And in memory of Murray J. Gart,
friend and inspiration since my childhood,
seeker of truth and promoter of understanding
about the Arab world.

CONTENTS

CONTENTS

PREFACE

What is it like, growing up in the Arab world today? Is life there as dangerous and difficult as it looks in our newspapers and on television? For some teenagers, in places of unusual tension and conflict, yes. But the lives of others will seem quite familiar to you, in many ways. What young people want is what young people everywhere want: a secure home and loving family, good friends, teachers who care about their students, the chance to grow and to express themselves, hope for a better future. Some other aspects of their existence—the land itself, history, the way people are ruled, beliefs and social customs—may strike you as surprising, certainly "different." Above all, young people in the Arab world share with young Americans the challenge of growing up in a complicated, confusing world, trying to meet life with courage, faith, and not least of all, humor. Let the teenagers in these stories tell you something about their lives.

ELSA MARSTON
FEBRUARY 15, 2008

ACKNOWLEDGMENTS

Although I have lived in or visited all the places described in these stories, the help of several friends in the Middle East and the United States was indispensable in bringing them to life. For an accurate description of Baghdad in 2000, I wish to thank again my Iraqi friends, Khadim Shaaban ("Uncle Omar") of Bloomington, Indiana, and Shaker Mustafa and Nawal Nasrallah in Boston. The comments of Richard Antoun, professor of anthropology at Binghamton State University, were most useful in the research for "Honor." Others who helped along the way include Loubna El-Amine, Helen Frost, Paula Sunderman, Amal Haddadin, and especially my son, Ramsay Harik. As always, I am beholden to my friends in the Bloomington Children's Authors—Elaine Marie Alphin, Marilyn Anderson, Pat McAlister, Keiko Kasza, Patricia Batey, Stuart Lowry, and Pamela Service. I'm delighted by filmmaker Raouf Zaki's faith in the cinematic potential of "Santa Claus in Baghdad," resulting in his film (RA Vision Productions) scheduled for 2008. The unfailing encouragement of Donald Gallo over the years has meant a lot to me. Finally, I shall always be grateful to George Braziller, and his editor Tara Zapp, for producing the earlier version of this book, *Figs and Fate: Stories About Growing Up in the Arab World Today;* and to Janet Rabinowitch of Indiana University Press for seeing the possibilities in a considerably expanded edition, the better to help young (and older!) Americans become acquainted with some "real life" people in the Arab world.

1

Santa Claus in Baghdad

A STORY FROM IRAQ (2000)

Amal listened gloomily to the little speech that Mr. Kareem had prepared. He spoke in a halting fashion, almost as though he were making an apology, but clearly he was as happy as a bird.

"And I know," he concluded, "that my students will greet their new teacher with respect and helpfulness, and will show how well Mr. Kareem has taught them about our glorious literary heritage." He laughed awkwardly at his little joke, and some of the girls responded with polite smiles.

A shy bachelor, Mr. Kareem inspired more respect than affection among his students. Many complained of his tough assignments and rigorous grading, although Amal thought he was quite fair. In any case, no one could deny that Mr. Kareem taught with competence and, in his stammering way, enthusiasm. He loved the works of the old poets and tried valiantly to convey to his students the richness of Arabic literature.

Another teacher leaving us, thought Amal. *How many—four this fall?*

But who could blame them? Anyone who had a chance at even a mediocre job somewhere else—*anywhere* that wasn't Iraq—

would be crazy not to grab it. At last something good had come Mr. Kareem's way, a job in one of the Gulf states, and he would be leaving as soon as the term ended in January.

Still, Amal couldn't help feeling let down. So few teachers these days taught with any commitment, she thought, or any love of learning. Whoever replaced Mr. Kareem would most likely be from the bottom of the jar. No one but a cockroach could live on what a teacher was paid. Good people always went away.

Then a brighter thought popped into Amal's head. For a change, someone good was *coming*! Uncle Omar, the famous relative from America, was due any day now, bringing things the family sorely needed and couldn't buy in Baghdad. Amal's mother kept talking about vitamins and nutritional supplements, while Bilaal, who had only the haziest idea who Uncle Omar was, chattered about the wonderful toys—cars and trucks and balloons. Amal, too, hoped there would be something more interesting than just vitamins. Yes, Uncle Omar was coming, and she could look forward to that.

But then he, too, would leave.

At the recess, the girls traipsed out to the school yard, gathered in little knots, and grumbled. Ordinarily Amal would have joined one of the quieter groups, but this time she drifted toward the girls who always clustered around Hala. Amal was curious as to what Hala might have to say about Mr. Kareem. Beautiful and confident at thirteen, Hala had something to say on any matter that came up.

"Mr. Kareem," she was declaring, her voice high and assertive, "has been teaching all the Arabic literature courses at this school for centuries. It's time for a change—like somebody young and handsome, right from the university. We could do with a little life in our classroom!"

"Is anybody studying Arabic literature at the university?" Rafeeka asked. "Is anybody studying anything?"

Hala hesitated, then rallied, a sparkle coming back to her pretty dark eyes. "Well, of course! The world has to go on, doesn't it? So we'll just go to the principal and tell her that we insist on a young, handsome teacher to take Mr. Kareem's place."

The girls laughed, and someone said, "Right. We don't care whether he knows anything about Arabic literature."

Poor Mr. Kareem, thought Amal. *He looks dopey, with his skinny shape and bony face, but he's a good teacher. I'd rather have a dopey-looking good teacher than somebody who looks good but doesn't know how to teach. And it's not Mr. Kareem's fault that he's so skinny.*

She wondered whether she'd have felt that way a year earlier, so ready to forgive a teacher for not being perfect. No, she'd been just as critical and gossipy as anyone else, before she got sick. Thinking of Mr. Kareem's skinniness reminded Amal of the way her own clothes had hung on her last spring. With no medicine available that her parents could afford, her bout with pneumonia had lasted nearly forever. She still recalled the shock when, starting to get better at last, she looked in the mirror for the first time. No color in her skin, hollow cheeks, eyes almost too big for her face . . . and her arms, which had formerly been so good at shooting baskets, hung like withered branches. How much weight had she lost—almost twenty pounds?

Now Amal was almost healthy again. But she'd had to repeat the year at school, and her place in the new group of girls had proved as awkward a fit as her dowdy, too-big clothes. Although a year older than most of her classmates, she had become a tagalong.

Just then, she caught sight of Mr. Kareem making his diffident way across the school yard. There was a short break in the chatter as others also noticed him. Suddenly Amal spoke, surprising herself as much as the others.

5

"I think we should give Mr. Kareem a gift." Seven or eight faces turned to her, as though she had broken some sort of rule.

"Why?" asked Hala. "To reward him for giving us such low grades?"

"He—he gives us the grades we earn," said Amal. "He's fair, you know."

A surge of energy went through her as she spoke. Maybe she sounded goody-goody, sticking up for the teacher like that, but she hadn't felt this sort of excitement for a long time. It was almost like the days before her illness, when *she* was the center of a circle and other girls looked up to her. In those days she had felt full of purpose and fun; she'd looked forward to whatever each new day could bring. That wasn't how she felt now.

But here she was, surprisingly, speaking out again—and others were listening to her! She went on, before she could lose her nerve.

"Mr. Kareem always tries hard—don't you think so? And he cares. He wants us to really like the stuff he's teaching."

Two or three girls muttered in agreement. "That's true. He's not so bad."

Encouraged, Amal spoke more firmly, though her heart seemed to be pounding. "And now he's leaving, and we probably *won't* get someone as good. We should honor him. It's an honor to honor a good teacher."

"Yes," said someone behind her. "That's what my father says. Amal's right."

At that, Hala resumed command. "Why, of course! I never said we shouldn't, did I? Naturally we'll give him a present. You always do that, for a good teacher."

Looking around, Amal saw that the others were nodding. Now that Hala had endorsed it, they would go along with the idea. Many students would be uneasy at the thought of having to chip in for a gift, as Amal was well aware, but Hala's friends came from well-off families, people with mysterious connections that brought them a comfortable income. These girls, Amal knew, had a few coins in their pockets.

"So," Hala continued, "let's decide what we're going to give our honored teacher. Well, somebody suggest something."

What, indeed, would be a good gift for a man? A few suggestions came forth, each to be shot down by one girl or another.

"A sweater, a shirt?" Too personal. Too expensive.

"A scarf?" Don't be dumb. In the Gulf he's going to need a *scarf*?

"Then a necktie? That old brown one he wears has *got* to go. Or maybe cologne?"

"A desk set—you know, with places for pens and paper clips."

Hala frowned at every suggestion but offered no ideas of her own. Then Amal heard herself speaking again.

"A book. I think we should give him a book. After all, he teaches literature."

"Books are so dull," objected Hala. "And I doubt that he'll want to lug a whole library around with him."

Rafeeka spoke up. "We don't have to give him a whole library, just one book. A nice one."

"A book is personal," said Amal, "but not *too* personal."

"Right. *I* vote for a book," said Rafeeka, with a theatrical toss of her curly hair. Several others echoed her.

Hala folded her arms and looked aside, as though giving the matter careful thought. Then she declared, "Okay, we'll give him a book. That's just what I was thinking of anyway. So we need a committee. Rafeeka, you and me and . . ."

As Hala hesitated again, Amal saw the door opening wider for her. This was her chance. She didn't have to stumble along forever behind these younger girls, who didn't even know as much as she did.

"I can choose a book," she said. "Anybody who wants to go with me, okay. But anyway, I can do it."

"You?" said Hala. "How do you know what kind of book Mr. Kareem would like?"

At this challenge, Amal felt another spark of her old fire. "Something to do with literature, of course. Shakespeare, or—or Tolstoy, one of those people. My family can help me. Actually, my grandfather taught literature at Baghdad University."

For a moment there was silence, as though everyone were waiting for someone else to speak. When no one did, and the other girls were looking expectantly at Amal, Hala spoke up with her usual authority. "All right, then, you do it. After all, what's so hard about buying a book? Does anybody want to go with Amal? Well, whoever wants to, can. Everybody bring some money tomorrow, or soon. Let's say a hundred dinars. We can all chip in that much, can't we?"

All right, thought Amal, *you run the show, Hala, until I get the money in my hands. Then I'll choose the book—and I'll make the presentation to Mr. Kareem.*

"Good," Amal said. "When we have enough money, I'll—and whoever else wants to—we'll go get a beautiful book. Something Mr. Kareem will like. We want him to leave with nice thoughts about us, don't we?"

"We want him to leave behind good grades for us!" said Hala, and all the girls laughed.

Timing would be important, Amal realized. Naturally Mr. Kareem would see through a bribe, so they would have to wait till the very last day of the term, after exams.

8

But something else worried her. A hundred dinars—that was a lot of money. Maybe not for Hala and her friends, but for Amal's parents—a bank clerk and an elementary-school teacher—it would be difficult. What had she gotten herself into?

Later that afternoon, Amal went off to pick up her little brother at his school. It was a long walk, and as usual she worried about being late. Almost seven, small and thin, Bilaal was a bright but anxious child. The slightest thing might throw him into a tizzy, and once he fixed on an idea, he would fret it to death. If he decided that his sister was not coming for him, he would probably refuse to believe she was there, even when she took him by the hand. Amal had to smile at the thought.

She reached the drab, decaying building with its small school yard, in which a single potted plant, puny and limp, provided the only beauty. Just as Amal feared, most of the children had already left and Bilaal was jumping up and down in a frenzy. Soon, though, she saw that the frenzy had nothing to do with her being late.

"He *is* coming, he *is* coming!" Bilaal squealed as he rushed up to Amal. "Isn't he, Amal? Dumb old Sami doesn't believe me, and I told everybody over and over. He *is* coming—tell them, Amal!"

Dumb old Sami, just leaving, tugged at his mother's hand and turned back. "It's not true," he insisted, making a face. "Bilaal is just telling stories."

A screech rose from Bilaal, and Sami's mother yanked her son away. At that moment one of the teachers came out to the playground. Amal, alarmed to see her brother working himself into a tantrum, turned to her for some explanation.

"I'm afraid we've had quite a time with Bilaal," the teacher said wearily, her shoulder-length reddish hair so tousled it looked as though she'd been through a battle. "I'd better tell you, so your mother can deal with it."

9

As Amal waited, half dreading what would happen next, the teacher took a deep breath and went on. "Somebody gave me a book for the children a few days ago. We have so few books, you know, and have had no new ones for years, so I was glad to get it. Maybe some relief organization sent it. Anyway, it's about Christmas, but it's not religious. It's about Santa Claus—Baba Noel. They call him Santa Claus in America—Santa Claus and his deer who pull a wagon through the sky and bring gifts for children. So I read it to the children, and they liked it and wanted to hear it again. And again, and again, and again. Maybe it was a mistake." She sighed.

"No, it's not a mistake, it's true!" Bilaal piped up, pulling at his sister's hand. "Tell her, Amal!"

The teacher smiled at him, a tired, hopeless smile, and paused as though uncertain how to continue with the story. Beginning to see connections, Amal tried to help.

"We have an uncle coming from America," she said. "Maybe that's what Bilaal is thinking of. He should be here tomorrow or the next day."

As the teacher's face cleared, Bilaal's grew redder. "*Santa Claus* is coming! He's bringing toys and presents for us—Mama told me. A red car! It's Santa Claus, Amal. Or just like him!"

Had Mama really promised Bilaal that Uncle Omar would have toys? Oh dear. But Amal could understand how Bilaal might have turned the eagerly awaited Uncle Omar into Santa Claus with a wagon full of toys. And when Bilaal got obsessed with something, he would pester relentlessly until Mama had to agree, just to save her sanity.

Besides, the kid had never had a new toy of his own . . . never, not for any holiday, not for his birthday. Toys were too expensive. One could live without toys. Any gift would have to be something practical: clothes or shoes, pencils, a school bag.

"I see," said the teacher, pulling her skimpy cardigan tighter in the chilly breeze. "Well, he insisted, and the other children didn't believe him. Of course they wanted to, but they didn't. So we've had a lot of arguing these last few days."

Amal tried to nod reassuringly. "It's all right. Yes, somebody's coming to us—Santa Claus or Baba Noel, or somebody just as good. Bilaal is right. He's bringing . . . good things." She couldn't quite say *toys*.

"Lucky you," muttered the teacher. As she started to go back inside the building, she paused. "So we won't talk about it anymore, all right, Bilaal? We understand now. Someone good is coming to you. But we mustn't talk about it, because then the other children will feel bad. Isn't that right?"

"Yes," said Bilaal, pacified. "Santa Claus," he added in a lower voice. "It's Santa Claus."

"Yes. And now we must hurry home, Bilaal," said Amal. "Mama will be waiting for us." They left the school yard and walked through the bleak streets, skirting puddles and trash. While relieved to have her brother calm once more, Amal was uneasy. Should she have let him go on thinking Santa Claus was coming, or correct him at the start? But then Bilaal would have gotten frantic again and driven his poor teacher out of her mind. What *should* she have done?

Anyway, he would get over this. He'd forget. Amal could only hope that Uncle Omar would have something nice for Bilaal . . . and some kind of medicine that would help him calm down.

Uncle Omar arrived in Baghdad and began to make the rounds among all the relatives. When it was her family's turn, Amal came home from school to find her mother in such a flurry of cooking as she hadn't seen in years.

"Mama," she said, "you have enough to do. Let me fry that eggplant."

Her mother half turned from the kerosene burner. "No, I'll do it. But you can tend the *lahm mishwi*. Don't let the meat get over-done—it'll be tough enough as it is."

With a handful of metal skewers and a plate of cutup meat and onions, Amal went out onto the small balcony, where a brazier stood. There was only scrap wood to burn—no charcoal—and it flared up and died down quickly. Tending both the erratic fire and the easily scorched kebabs would keep Amal busy.

She had tried to discourage her mother from making too many dishes. Surely the other family who was coming would bring some-thing, wouldn't they? But Mama was determined. Whatever she could do for Omar, her own first cousin, was not half good enough! It would be a disgrace not to have a fine meal for him. After all, he had been going to a different family's home each night since his arrival four days earlier, and every family had done their best. She wasn't going to be outdone by her sisters, certainly not! Never mind that tonight's feast would mean lentils for the next month.

The challenge of making so little go so far, however, was taking a toll on Amal's mother. She was nervous and fatigued. Small won-der, Amal thought, what with teaching all afternoon, then standing in line at the butcher's, then rushing home to prepare one dish after another. And all on that wretched kerosene burner—the gas stove having died years ago. Mama worried constantly about the danger of fire. That was why, as Amal knew, she had wanted her daughter out of the kitchen while the eggplant was sputtering away in hot oil.

When the meat was broiled and giving off a fragrance that belied its toughness, Amal brought it inside. "What now, Mama? Prepare the place for eating?"

Her mother looked pained for a moment. The heavy dining table had been sold, so now the family ate around a plastic cloth spread on the living room floor. At first Amal and Bilaal had pretended it was a picnic, but the idea soon lost its charm.

Then, "Yes, for ten," said Amal's mother. "Fareeda and Shamam and their three kids, and Omar, and us. When you've finished, try to find something to do with your brother. Keep him calm. I don't want him all worked up by the time Omar gets here."

To Amal's surprise, Bilaal had not said anything more about Santa Claus since the scene at school. His teacher said he seemed to understand that he should not gloat about nice things. And maybe he had forgotten. Amal decided it was best that she hadn't reported the Santa Claus incident, which would only have added to her mother's anxieties.

To keep Bilaal from getting too excited, nonetheless, Amal and her parents had been saying little about Uncle Omar's visit. That wasn't easy, because everyone else in the family, all the aunts and uncles and their families, had immediately reported on Omar's three overweight suitcases and bulging overcoat pockets. Amal hoped he would have some little gifts—a pretty hair clasp, a pair of good socks, maybe even a blouse—and wished she could chatter happily about her expectations. But she kept her mouth shut.

At last, dinner was ready and Uncle Omar arrived, winded from climbing up to the fourth floor. Papa came right behind him, lugging a large suitcase. Uncle Omar looked very weary. Reddened eyes, heavy cheeks, stains on his gray sweater, no tie . . . to Amal he didn't look much like a rich uncle from America. But the shouts and hugs and kisses quickly swept away her disapproval. Mama was so happy to see him she couldn't stop patting his face. "Allah, ten years, dear one, ten years!" she kept crying.

After shoving the suitcase into a bedroom, Papa seized the visitor's arms, kissed him repeatedly on both cheeks, thumped his back. Uncle Omar's tired face brightened and his eyes filled with tears as he kissed Amal and Bilaal.

When Aunt Fareeda and Uncle Shamam arrived with their three children, all older than Amal, the hugging, kissing, and shouting started all over again. Amal felt her throat tighten and her eyes grow watery in the flood of emotion. She didn't notice Bilaal's attempts to get her attention until he'd tugged at her arm several times.

When at last she bent down to hear him, he whispered stealthily, eyeing the newcomer. "He doesn't look like he's supposed to, Amal. Why doesn't he look the way he's supposed to?"

For a moment she was puzzled: how did Bilaal know what Uncle Omar was supposed to look like? Then, understanding, she tried desperately to think of a quick answer. Yes, the pictures of Baba Noel, or Santa Claus, or whatever he was called, showed him in a red coat. Something like that.

Pulling Bilaal to a corner of the room, she squatted down to get closer to him. "Those are just his traveling clothes, Bilaal," she murmured. "He can't wear his good clothes, his *right* clothes, all the time. They probably need cleaning."

"No," Bilaal whispered back. "I mean he doesn't have his beard."

"Oh, that! He shaved it off. Sometimes men do. They think a beard is nice for a while, and then they get tired of it."

Bilaal looked at her dubiously. "But he's not . . ." At that moment one of his teenaged cousins swept him up in her arms and started showing him off to Uncle Omar. Amal caught one last questioning glance from her brother. He then turned his attention back toward his welcoming admirers. Evidently Bilaal had decided to be amiable, at least for the time being.

14

Mama's dinner, everyone proclaimed, was a miracle, and Amal was happy to see her mother laughing with pleasure. The fried eggplant was seasoned to perfection, the broiled meat excellent, the fried potatoes crisp, the salad savory. Wonderful oranges, better than any since nobody-knew-when! As for dessert . . . well, nothing much—until Uncle Omar produced a jar of fig jam he'd picked up in the airport in Jordan. Fig jam and bread—what more does one need for sweets?

At last the time came to see what else Uncle Omar had brought. Papa pulled the suitcase out into the sitting room, and everyone sat or knelt as their guest opened it. Amal held Bilaal in her lap. He was alert and eager, but said nothing.

Item by item, out came the contents of the suitcase. Bottles, boxes, jars . . . pills, capsules, tablets . . . reading glasses, bandages, corn plasters, scissors . . . ointments, creams, salves. A whole pharmacy, a king's ransom in medicines, lay before them. *Open, Sesame!* The wonders poured forth in their tubes, packets, and syringes.

A hushed atmosphere had fallen over the room, after the loud chatter and laughter at dinner. The adults watched closely as Uncle Omar brought forth each new treasure, and they greeted his announcements with appreciative murmurs. The young people soon lost interest and sat back in their chairs, waiting patiently for the display to finish. It was pretty hard to scream with joy about calcium, thought Amal, or faint with delight over aspirin—even if you hadn't been able to get it for years.

All this while, Bilaal sat quietly on her lap without speaking. Yet she could feel the tension rippling through his small body as he leaned forward. Every move that Uncle Omar made, he watched intently. Every item lifted from the suitcase, he stared at as though his life depended on it.

15

When the treasure was finally all revealed, Uncle Omar sat back and his features relaxed in a smile. "I couldn't bring presents for the children," he said. "Not enough room, not with all this. And how do I know what they like? But I know the children can use a little money. From their auntie and me." With quick gestures he handed Amal and her three cousins each a couple of bills, then turned to give something to Amal's father. "For the little one," he said.

The older children received their gifts with quiet thanks. No pretty hair clasps, no blouses . . . but as Amal stole a glance at the bills in her hand, she caught her breath. Uncle Omar had not been stingy.

Suddenly, in the hush that still filled the room, a small voice spoke. "I want a car. A red one. A racing car."

One of the boy cousins gave a short laugh, but everyone else turned to Bilaal in surprise. He repeated his demand.

"Where's my car? Where are the toys? Santa Claus has toys! He doesn't have just—just this stuff! I want a red racing car. Please, give me my red racing car!"

"But, dear one," said Mama, coming over to him, "Uncle Omar wasn't able to bring any cars. He had to—to bring other things instead."

"A car wouldn't fit into that little suitcase," said Papa with a forced laugh.

Bilaal slid off Amal's knees, facing her and his mother. "You promised! You said Santa Claus was coming and would bring me toys! Where are they?"

Amal felt a wave of cold dismay go through her. Yes, she should have told, after all! She shouldn't have taken the easy way out and agreed with him, back on that fateful day at his school. But how could she have known how seriously he would take it?

Uncle Omar stammered with embarrassment. "I don't have a car, but I have—I have—" He rummaged through his pockets and pulled out a box of Chiclets. "I have this for you!"

Bilaal looked at the Chiclets, as though surprised that Santa Claus could make such a dumb mistake. "I want toys," he said. "I want a car!"

"Enough, Bilaal." Now his mother spoke sternly. "There are no cars. There are only things we need—"

Suddenly the anticipation that had been simmering inside Bilaal exploded. He threw himself on the floor, cried and shouted, pounded his fists. Amal made a grab for him, hoping to pick him up and comfort him, but caught a sharp kick and backed off. Others tried to gather up the treasures from Uncle Omar's suitcase, all those precious medicines and nutrients that had squeezed out the toys, to save them from the thrashing of Bilaal's body. Totally out of control, Bilaal screamed and blubbered, beating anything within reach.

Amal's mother fumbled frantically among the medicines until she found a bottle and opened it. "Amal," she gasped, "a spoon."

A medicine for Bilaal's yelling spells, Amal hoped. No, just cough syrup—but maybe there was something in it that would calm him down.

While her mother held the thrashing child, Amal managed to get a spoonful of liquid into his mouth. Before long his writhing subsided a bit, enough for his mother to take him into the bedroom and close the door.

As the screams and sobs grew fainter, a quiet dismay settled on everyone in the sitting room. Then Aunt Fareeda gathered her share of the treasure and announced, with a brave attempt at sweetness, that her family must be leaving.

17

"I'm sorry," Uncle Omar kept murmuring throughout the good-byes. "I didn't realize. . . . I should have brought something. . . ."

"No!" Papa said, blustering through his chagrin. "We beg your forgiveness. What can we say? It is a shame, a disgrace. I don't un-derstand—I have no idea why the boy should act like that. What a shame! He will be punished."

No, he won't be, Amal thought. *Papa can't bear to punish his only son. And it's more my fault, really. I should have talked to Bilaal. . . . I should have told Mama. Poor thing, hoping and expecting so hard, and nothing came true. He's still too young to have learned that you can't expect* anything. *Not in this world.*

Amal didn't see Uncle Omar again. Her parents went to visit with him at the relatives' houses, not daring to risk another en-counter between Bilaal and the failed Santa Claus. Then he left. Amal was sorry not to have seen more of him, as he had seemed like a nice man. He was not very smart about bringing things for little kids, but he had tried to do the right thing. She would write him a thank-you letter.

The night after Uncle Omar's departure, Amal noticed that her father had a secret look about him, a look of suppressed eagerness. After the evening meal of lentils and rice, and before Bilaal's bed-time, Papa called the boy to him.

"Bilaal," he said, bending over a little, "something wonderful has happened. Our visitor . . . Uncle Omar, you remember him? Well, he—he had a surprise for you. He couldn't find it in the big suitcase he brought—"

Oh Papa, thought Amal. *Be careful.*

"—it was such a big suitcase, you know, and something got lost with all the other things he had. But then he found it, and—here it is!" With a shaky smile, Papa brought his hand from behind his back. There, resting on his palm, was a little red car. A sports car, bright, shiny red, and, so far as Amal could see, brand new. It lay like a jewel in Papa's hand, gleaming in the light of the one bulb overhead.

For a long moment Bilaal simply stared. Tentatively, then, he reached for the car. Holding it like a sacred object, he examined it from every angle. He looked up at his father. "Did Uncle Omar get it from Santa Claus?" he asked in a hushed voice. "Did Santa Claus give it to Uncle Omar?"

"Well, I'm not sure just what—but I think so."

"For me? Especially for me?"

"Yes, it's for you, Bilaal."

"Mama!" Bilaal shouted in a sudden burst. "Mama, come see! Santa Claus *did* give me a car, he did, he did!"

His mother came from the kitchen, and they all watched as Bilaal dropped to his knees and started chugging the little car around on the living room floor. "Baroom, baroom, baroom! Eeeeee—BAROOM!" Bilaal was beside himself with joy. There would be no bedtime for him until he fell asleep from happy exhaustion.

Amal, her heart full, glanced at her parents as they watched him. Her father's face shone with moisture. Perspiration or tears? She wasn't sure which. His expression reminded Amal of the masks of drama, which she had seen pictured in a book about plays. Tragedy and comedy, both. Sometimes comedy and tragedy weren't all that far apart.

Her mother's face showed no emotion, just a slight upturning at the corners of the mouth. After a moment, the two adults exchanged a look and a few murmured words that Amal barely caught over the automotive racket.

"Well, there. Let's hope it lasts."

"A man has to—to make his child happy. How can I deny him everything?"

The words brought back to Amal another conversation she had overheard between them. As Bilaal went on flinging himself about noisily, chugging the car, she tried to recall what she had heard, two nights earlier. She'd been in her room trying to study for exams. Her parents, in their bedroom, seemed agitated about something, and bits of their discussion had reached her through the walls. Yes, it was coming back.

"How could you?" her mother had said, her voice rising. "Those books—you know what they meant to your father!"

"What else was there? There's nothing—"

"It's unbearable—I can't even think of it. Look, if you must do this, then at least get him something he needs—"

"Needs? He needs everything! Omar's money will go for that. This I must do myself. My son hasn't had a new toy in his whole life! I can't face myself. A man can't deny his only son every little bit of happiness, can he? It was bad enough, having Omar think I couldn't . . . I had to do it, by God!"

At the time, Amal had shut it out of her mind. She had heard these discussions before, as her parents agreed to get along without something else that they didn't really need . . . the silver, china, pressure cooker, the carpets, embroidered tablecloths—and of course, the dining table. She hadn't wanted to hear any more. Besides, she had to study. Mr. Kareem would give a tough exam, and she wanted to do her best.

But now the meaning of those bitter words hit her. Papa had taken more books from the remains of the family library and had sold them to one of the men who peddled books in the street. One of that long, long line of people who sold second-hand goods in the flea market . . . rather, who *offered* them for sale. Because who could buy, Amal often wondered, if nobody could afford to keep their books any longer?

But happily, that sad thought reminded her of a brighter one. *She* could buy a book! She was one of the lucky ones who could go to the book market to buy, not just to sell. And she must do it soon, because Mr. Kareem would be leaving right after exams. Tomorrow she would get the money from President-and-Treasurer Hala, and then she would go looking for the perfect book.

On the next-to-last day of the term, after school, Amal set out on her quest. Hala had grandly presented her with the money collected from the class. "Rafeeka and Naila are bringing sweets instead," she'd added. "I told them to. We have to have some nice refreshments, after all."

Now, as Amal walked through the downtown streets, she counted the money for the third time. Her own parents had contributed willingly, as much as they could. She was glad of that. It would have been awful if she hadn't been able to put in her share. Still, she wasn't sure whether the money would be enough for a gift-worthy book.

Her first stop was the only bookstore she knew about that might have new books. She was soon disappointed. The owner had little more than drab books in Russian. With a sigh, Amal headed for the open-air stalls of the flea market.

Looking straight ahead, she walked quickly past the displays of household goods. She didn't want to risk seeing something she recognized, covered with street dust . . . her mother's silver serving tray, or perhaps that lovely painting of an English countryside from Aunt Fareeda's sitting room.

At least books were more anonymous, she thought. Most of them wouldn't have quite the same aura of having been cherished and admired. But as Amal reached the streets where books were sold, she let out a gasp of dismay. So many! So many, many books! Table after table after table covered with books, and a row of upright display stands that stretched as far as she could see. How could she ever search through so many books to find the right one?

And the booksellers . . . shabby, listless men who looked totally uninterested in their wares, who probably didn't know one book from another. Well, how could they? They were just trying to eke out a living, miserable as it was.

Resolutely, Amal started down the book-lined street. She saw lots of religious books, all in Arabic. Sadder to see, she thought, were the innumerable books about medicine and medical studies, in English and other foreign languages. How could doctors know how to treat people if they couldn't keep their books? And there were thousands more books on all subjects—history, sociology, science, computer technology. Some were in good condition, but most were smudged and dog-eared paperbacks.

As she gazed at the street full of knowledge that nobody could afford any longer, Amal seemed to hear her teacher's voice. Mr. Kareem had told the class so many times about the great days when their city of Baghdad was the center of learning for the whole world. A thousand years ago, at the height of Islamic civilization, the libraries of Baghdad had brought together books from as far away as Spain and China. Scholars, too, had come from all over the known world to bring books and to study, copy, and translate the treasured volumes in Baghdad's "House of Wisdom." Books and Baghdad were practically synonymous.

Amal remembered the proud ring of Mr. Kareem's words. Then came the sadness in his voice, on those days when he told the rest of the story. The glorious era had ended in total destruction. Hordes from Central Asia had come sweeping overland in the thirteenth century . . . men who, as Mr. Kareem put it, were scarcely more civilized than the horses they rode upon. In those dreadful days the streets of Baghdad had run red with blood, while the great Tigris River ran blue—blue with the ink of books.

And now, Amal thought, here were the libraries of Baghdad, right before her eyes . . . fading in the sun and wind and in the rain that brought down indelible splotches from the dust in the air.

She walked past table after table. Were there no books about Arabic literature? Yes, here and there a cheap-looking, battered novel—not the sort of book that she thought Mr. Kareem would value. She spotted some books of literary criticism, but they looked dismal. How could you give somebody a book that you had no admiration for yourself? Maybe she should look for something in English, since Mr. Kareem had studied English literature as well as Arabic.

Finally Amal came to a bookseller who didn't look quite like the others. Frayed and stoop-shouldered, true, but there was something more about him, something that suggested he had greatly valued books in his past. Maybe he could help her.

"I'm looking for a book of literature," she told him. "For a gift."

"Your teacher?" When she nodded, the man rubbed his unshaven chin thoughtfully. "I have some here. You look around."

Amal noticed a whole set of books by an English man named Thomas Hardy, and a book by one of the old Greeks, and of course several volumes by Shakespeare. So there were possibilities here. But Mr. Kareem undoubtedly had Shakespeare, and how could she know which other books would be special for him, when she had barely even heard of writers such as Hemingway and Dickens?

Now she began to regret the bold claim she had made back in the school yard. How had she dared say that she, better than any-

23

one else, could choose the perfect book? She had wanted so much to impress Hala's crowd. . . . But the job was turning out to be a lot harder than she'd expected.

At long last Amal narrowed her choice to two books, a thick one with a whale on the cover—it looked serious in spite of the whale—and a collection of poems by a man named Robert Frost. She opened the book of poems and found that they were short and not too hard to read. Mr. Kareem might like them.

But just as she was ready to make up her mind, the bookseller picked up another volume that she hadn't noticed. "Here, have a look at this. It's more than you can pay, but just have a look, miss."

It was a beautiful book, truly beautiful, the tooled leather cover embossed in faded gold, in Arabic. Opening it to a place in the middle, Amal delicately touched the pages, which were trimmed with gold edges. The paper was so heavy it felt almost like fabric, and the printed letters seemed to flow like silken threads. The pages had decoration, with rich colors painted by hand. Was it a Koran? Korans could be breathtakingly beautiful, Amal knew. But this was too thin a volume. No, it must be poetry.

She read the name on the cover. Abu Nawwas. She knew that name. Her class had studied some poems by Abu Nawwas. Even though written many hundreds of years ago, it was lovely poetry, Amal thought. And Mr. Kareem—why, Mr. Kareem *adored* it. When he talked about Abu Nawwas, his absolute favorite, he completely forgot his shyness and went into flights of ecstasy.

This was the book, then. It was beautiful, special, and held the poems of Abu Nawwas, which Mr. Kareem loved above all others. She would have to buy it.

"It's expensive," said the bookseller sadly. "I have to charge a decent price for it. This is a rare book, over a hundred years old. I'm sorry, miss."

Amal did a quick reckoning in her head. The amount collected from her classmates was about half of what the book would cost. She might bargain, try to get the man to lower his price a little. But already the price was far below what the book was worth—look at all that gold! It wouldn't be right to haggle.

"I . . ." Amal gulped, then forced out the words. "I want this book. I don't have enough money, but I will try to get more. Please, don't sell it to anybody else. I'll come back tomorrow."

She handed the book back to the bookseller, who gave a slight shrug as he fitted it into a slot. Plainly he didn't expect to sell that book, or perhaps any other, any time soon. As she walked away, Amal could almost feel him watching her, shaking his head in resignation.

But where would she get the money that she had so rashly promised? There was no way that she—or even Hala—could round up enough money from the other girls. Certainly her parents could not pay the difference. How embarrassing to have promised to get the "perfect book" and then have to admit that she couldn't! Amal could think of only one possible solution. It lurked in her mind like an unwelcome guest who would have to be accepted with feigned warmth.

The money that Uncle Omar had given her—Amal's own gift money—would make up the difference. No, it wasn't fair. Not at all fair that she should take responsibility for getting the present, and then end up paying so much more than her share. But what else could she do?

Amal sighed, and her eyes stung as she hurried back through the flea market, past all the tables of books, kitchenware, baby clothing, jewelry, furniture, toys, watches, blind television sets, and dead computers. It would have been so nice to have a new blouse, or a pair of shoes that wouldn't wear out too soon.

25

Amal attended school in the afternoon session, which just barely gave her time to return to the book market the next day. She had to hustle, but she arrived at school triumphant, with the precious volume in her book bag and the scene of her second encounter with the bookseller still bubbling in her head.

How astonished the old man had been to see her suddenly pop up at his stand! And then, when he heard her say she wanted the poems of Abu Nawwas—and held out a torn envelope with all the money in it—well, she knew she would never forget the look on his face. That in itself was a story.

He'd wrapped it in brown paper that was only a bit crumpled. Amal had begged the man not to use old newspaper, and he had agreed that this book deserved better. All the while, as he folded and smoothed the paper around the book with loving deliberation, then pressed a stamp on it to show that the purchase had come from his stall, she'd been hopping with impatience. But he wouldn't be hurried . . . it seemed to Amal as though he'd rather have had the book than the money! At last he presented it to her, with a smile so sweet and a bow so gracious that Amal had almost wanted to hug him.

Reaching the school building, strands of her hair flying loose and her heart racing with excitement, Amal went up the stairs two at a time to her classroom. She could hardly believe she was able to move so fast—Mama would be worried if she knew! Where had that energy come from? Surely, from feeling so happy! Seconds before the bell, she squeezed into her seat and grinned at the girl next to her.

Their Arabic literature exam, a few days earlier, had not been too hard. Maybe Mr. Kareem was giving *them* a going-away present, Amal thought; or maybe she'd been better prepared. As soon as the corrected exams were in their hands, the students began to relax. Tension broke into chatter, and Hala slithered over to Amal's desk.

"Well, have you got it? Did you remember?" she whispered.

"Yes, it's in my book bag. And it's—it's good."

Hala shot her a faintly skeptical glance. "Okay. Then I'm going to announce the party, right now."

As Mr. Kareem made his way to the front of the class, Hala stood up in her customary pose of authority. Amal tried to struggle out of her seat—it was broken and tilted too close to the desk. At last, awkwardly, she got to her feet and stood in the aisle near Hala, clutching her book bag. Mr. Kareem turned, with a look of surprise at finding that the girls, although dismissed, were all still there.

"Mr. Kareem," announced Hala in ringing tones, "we are sorry you are leaving, and so we have arranged a little party for you. No music or dancing, but some very nice sweets. Rafeeka and Naila, are they ready?"

Rafeeka brought a tray of small pastries, which Hala took from her and, with a grand gesture, offered to Mr. Kareem. As the sweets then made their way around the room, Hala continued her presentation.

"We also have gift for you, Mr. Kareem, so you can remember us. We all thought a long time about what would be best, and we decided—let's have it, Amal."

Having pulled the brown-wrapped package from her bag, Amal stepped forward. "We decided," she said before Hala could continue, "that this—this sort of thing would probably be best. I hope—we all hope—you will like it." She held out the package.

Mr. Kareem's eyes widened in surprise, magnified by his glasses. Hesitantly he accepted the offering, with mumbled thanks. Then noticing the bookseller's stamp on the brown paper, he murmured,

"Yes, I knew that man. He always had good quality." He started to open the package, taking his time, fumbling but respectful, in just the same way as the bookseller had when wrapping it. At last he held the fine, slim volume in his hands. Watching closely, for an instant Amal recalled the moment when Bilaal first beheld the magnificent red car.

"*Allah!*" Mr. Kareem breathed. "My God . . . Abu Nawwas! It is wonderful . . . beautiful. *Beautiful!* What can I say? This is from the class, from all of you?"

Several voices answered in unison, as the girls clustered around to look at the book.

"But, how could you?" he asked. "This is worth—How did you find such a thing?"

Rafeeka spoke. "Amal said she could—"

"I—I just . . . went shopping," Amal stammered. She certainly couldn't *say* she found that precious book in the street market, even though he must know. "I looked around, and finally I found this. I remembered you talked about Abu Nawwas a lot, and we read some of his poems."

Mr. Kareem's bony fingers traced the exquisite tooling on the cover, stroked the gold on the edge of the pages. His voice shook as he spoke. "It's too beautiful. I never thought in my life to own such a book. I thank you, my class, with all my heart!"

Amal sensed the eyes of her classmates turning to her, and dimly she heard the murmurs. Yes, they were pleased and impressed, and Amal felt her own heart swelling.

"We're glad you like it, Mr. Kareem," said Hala, raising her voice.

"Oh, yes! Oh, I like it so very much," he whispered, still overcome.

Gradually the other girls finished the sweets, said good-bye to their teacher, and left. Amal and Hala lingered.

"I saw some other nice books," Amal said hesitantly, "and I nearly chose something modern, a book of poetry by a man with a funny English name. But when I saw this beautiful cover and read the title—"

"Yes, yes, yes! You could not have chosen better." Mr. Kareem started to turn the pages one by one, touching each as though it were made of rare silk. Carefully he separated two that apparently had been stuck together by moisture or the gold leaf on the edges. Then, as he spread out the pages, he paused and peered more closely. A frown came over his thin features. Amal wondered. What could he have found that puzzled or displeased him?

"Ohhh," murmured Mr. Kareem. "Oh, the shame of it—the tragedy!"

"What?" asked Hala. "What's wrong with the book? Amal, why didn't you—"

Flustered, Amal tried to say something, but Mr. Kareem broke in. "There is nothing wrong with the book . . . except that it's in my hands. This book belonged—" he swallowed, audibly— "it belonged to my professor at the university. A superb scholar, an excellent teacher, a wonderful man . . . how he must have treasured this book. And now his family has had to sell it. It would have broken his heart to know. . . . Look. Here is his name."

He held out the book so that the two girls could see the signature on the title page. Hala glanced at it and, finding no particular tragedy there, gave a little shrug.

But Amal's gaze was instantly fixed by what she saw, and she caught her breath in astonishment. There, in elegant handwriting, was her grandfather's name. Suddenly, everything became clear.

Abu Nawwas equaled a little red car. The jewel of her grandfather's library had gone to make Bilaal happy, to help a little boy believe that good things could sometimes happen . . . that Santa Claus would not completely forget the children of Baghdad.

With wide eyes, Amal looked up at Mr. Kareem, and they held each other's gaze for a moment. Yes, she thought, he understands.

Then Mr. Kareem said in a quiet voice, "I wish I could return this to the family of that great man."

Amal felt torn by conflicting feelings—the shame of her family at having had to sell the book, the miracle of her finding it, and the joy of seeing what it meant to her teacher. Searching for the right words, at last she said softly, "Maybe someday. But anyway, I think they'd be happy to know that the book is with you, our teacher."

"For now, I am honored to keep it," he said.

As the two girls left the classroom, Amal was scarcely aware of Hala's chatter, which drifted past her like mist off the Tigris. She was treasuring the images that lingered in her mind . . . the book resting in Mr. Kareem's thin fingers, the red car firmly clutched in Bilaal's little hand.

2

Faces

A STORY FROM SYRIA

Shifting uneasily on the velvet-cushioned divan, Suhayl surveyed the grand reception room. This was his first visit to the Turkish bath, a treat from his father. Upon his arrival he had been awed by the ancient building with its floors of colored tiles, the marble fountain, and peacocks painted on the walls—almost like a palace, he thought, where wonderful things might happen. As for the bath part, in some mysterious inner chambers he'd taken a good hot shower and then gotten dressed quickly, while his father went through the whole process: thumping massage, thorough scrubbing, and a final dip in cool water.

Now the time had come to talk. Suhayl shot a furtive glance at his father. Even now, he tried to hold on to a few wisps of hope. Maybe . . . maybe Papa would say he was coming home. In spite of the anger that had simmered inside Suhayl for months, he still longed for those days when they'd been a family, when his father and mother had both been there for him.

But Papa was in no hurry to talk, it seemed. With shiny, reddened skin and slicked-back hair, he lounged in a white terrycloth bathrobe and smoked a water pipe. Late afternoon sunlight, falling through colored glass in the dome high above them, made patterns on the white robe and on his face, like a mask. Suhayl thought his father a good-looking man, still slim and straight even though he had two grown-up sons in addition to Suhayl. But Suhayl did not want to look at his father long. He had little confidence in what might lie behind that handsome face.

"Well, son, how do you find it here?"

"It's nice," said Suhayl quietly. "It's beautiful." *Come on, tell me! Why did you really bring me here?*

"When you're older, you can come to the bath any time you want. It's good for you. Healthy. Relaxing. And cheap."

I said I liked it. Now, what about you? Are you coming back to us, or what?

Papa cleared his throat once, twice. "So, how's your mother?"

"All right." *Sure, we're doing fine by ourselves, just fine. Terrific. But—*

"Good." Puffing, Suhayl's father let a few minutes pass. Hitching around to a new position, he continued. "Huda and I are getting married next month. When we're settled, you'll come and live with us."

Suhayl sat motionless, as rigid as the stone arches overhead, his mind numb. Then his thoughts started churning. *I knew this was coming, sooner or later. I should've gone to live with you months ago . . . after my twelfth birthday. Sure, I know I'm only on loan to Mama, because you were being so generous, letting her hang on to me a little longer. . . . And besides, you like your freedom, don't you? You've been in no hurry to have a kid on your hands. Well, thanks a million. But of course I knew it couldn't go on much longer.*

"You'll like Huda," Suhayl's father was saying. "She's a lovely woman. Beautiful. Look, here's her picture." He pulled an envelope from the pocket of his bathrobe and took out a photo.

Suhayl glanced at it, then looked down again at his nervously clenched hands.

"Keep it, I brought it for you," said his father, putting the photo on the divan beside Suhayl. "Don't you think she's pretty?"

"Yes," mumbled Suhayl. After a moment, still with downcast eyes, he said, "My mother is beautiful, too."

Setting down the mouthpiece of the water pipe, his father straightened up and then awkwardly laid a hand on Suhayl's shoulder. "Yes, of course. But . . . well, my son, you'll understand later. It's better this way."

Taking a long stretch, he stood and went back to the dressing rooms. When he was out of sight, Suhayl tore the photo to bits and pushed them under the divan cushion.

Soon they were ready to leave. Suhayl climbed the well-worn steps to the entrance at street level, into the chill of a November afternoon. He felt as though he were being dragged from a refuge of beauty and comfort. But on second thought, the palace had not proved to be magical after all; no good news had awaited him there.

Suhayl and his father walked through the narrow alleys of uneven, foot-polished stones, the medieval passageways of the old part of Damascus. Emerging into a modern street, they found Papa's car parked nearby . . . a car as shiny and well cared for, Suhayl thought, as his father.

A large poster covered the wall above the car. Suhayl's father glanced at it and then turned away, frowning. "Our esteemed father," he muttered. "Always watching over us."

Suhayl, too, looked up at the face that loomed high on every street corner and on the fronts of buildings throughout the city—a face that appeared everywhere, even in the Turkish bath. He had seen it so often that he had long since stopped noticing. Now, however, he took another look. The president, with doves flying around his head . . . a face that looked kind and thoughtful, with a benign smile, as though he truly loved taking care of all the people in Syria.

"Our esteemed father, always watching," Papa had said about the president. Again Suhayl stole a look at his father. *Well, what is a father supposed to do? Isn't he supposed to watch over his family—and want them to be happy?*

His father opened the car door, turning to smile, and Suhayl wished he could return a smile of simple happiness and trust. Instead, with tightened jaw, he ducked his head and slid quickly into the front seat.

When he reached the flat, his mother was already there. Suhayl avoided making conversation. What could he tell her, after all, about the afternoon with his father? Fortunately, she had no questions. He barely glanced at her during supper, then quickly settled down with his homework.

Later that evening, however, while heading for the bathroom, Suhayl caught sight of his mother in her room. She was sitting at the dressing table, her back to him, and it was her reflection in the mirror that grabbed his attention.

He remembered painfully the way her appearance had changed in the months before his father left. A few times he had glimpsed her as she argued with her husband. Their voices were rarely raised, but the bitterness in his mother's face stuck in Suhayl's memory and choked his heart. He had asked himself, how could she be the same mother he had always known? *That* mother, whose dark eyes had rested on him so warmly, who had sung in the kitchen as she prepared the evening meal . . . where had she gone?

Silently Suhayl watched his mother. Her hair looked youthfully black in the dim light of her bedroom, but it was, he knew, beginning to show silver. *You look too tired, Mama, much older than you should.* Then she lifted her eyes and for an instant met his. Quickly her face seemed to grow firm again.

"Have you finished your studies, Suhayl? Do you need any help?"

"I'm done. I'm getting ready for bed now." Stepping hastily into the small bathroom, Suhayl began to splash water on his face, recklessly, as though cold water might wash away the images in his mind. He shivered as he left the bathroom, thinking at first it was from the drenching he'd given the front of his pajamas.

No . . . it's because everything's sad here. The whole place is soaked in sadness.

He hated to think of the days and weeks stretching on like this. His mother tried to be cheerful and make their lives move along as much as possible in the old way: he knew she did. But it was as futile as trying to bottle the first fragrance of spring.

Was there anything *he* could do? As he lay in bed, staring up at the pale patch on the ceiling thrown from the streetlight outside his window, Suhayl tried to think. There was no way he could bring his father back, now that Papa was going to marry that Huda lady. With a malicious little grin he thought of the scraps of photo under the divan cushion at the Turkish baths.

Too bad I didn't know some magic spell to put on that photo, so she'd just disappear. But when I'm living with them, they'll see. I'll have to keep a polite look on my face, but I'll find ways to show them how I really feel. . . .

Well, never mind that. What could he do for his mother, right now? How could he bring a smile back to her face, if only for a little while?

She used to look happy even when she returned home, tired from work. Her job with a construction company, doing something called "accounts," never sounded like much fun to Suhayl, but it had seemed to please her. His father, who received a good salary, had let her spend most of her earnings on clothes for herself and Suhayl.

Now, however, the money she earned had to stretch much further. She worked longer hours and looked exhausted when she got home, dropping into the armchair, kicking off her high heels, closing her eyes. Then after a few minutes she'd heave a big sigh, pull herself out of the chair, and go to the kitchen to start supper.

As all mothers did, of course. They had to feed their families, after all.

But dinner wasn't as good as it used to be, and they had the same things over and over again. His mother didn't seem to put much effort into making a nice meal anymore. Maybe it was hard, cooking dinner after working all day.

Suhayl began to think. Did it always have to be that way? She might sometime like a little change.

So . . . maybe . . . Suhayl could make dinner for her one night! Yes—why not? He'd have it all ready when she got home, so she wouldn't have to cook anything. What about this Friday night? A secret, of course, to surprise her! And she could rest and be happy. The tired lines in her face would soften, and she would smile at him.

Next morning, it still seemed like a good idea. Friday . . . that would give him five days to get ready. And maybe he could try to do a little better at school, too. Pay closer attention, so the teacher wouldn't complain . . . that dumb teacher who looked like a dried fig. Taught like a fig, too. Anyway, Suhayl would try harder, because he couldn't bear to think of the look his mother would give him if he brought home bad marks again.

After bolting down his breakfast, Suhayl hurried to the bus stop. The bus, when it finally came, was not too full, and he managed to wedge himself into a seat where he could look at the people near him. Recalling his father's masklike face in the colored light of the baths, and the treacherous smile of the beautiful Huda, he began to wonder about the faces around him. Brown, ruddy, pale, some smooth as a sweet white apricot, some wrinkled as a prune . . . all different. But *they* all probably hid stories, too.

That fat man with half-shut eyes and pudgy cheeks—did he eat too much because he was greedy, or because it was the only thing he could enjoy in life? And that young woman, whose eyes darted constantly from one side to the other . . . what was she afraid of seeing?

All those faces probably hide the truth, things they don't want other people to know. I'll bet every face does. Mine, too.

At school the day went quickly, for once. Math was easy. Finishing his work Suhayl decided to write down, on a corner of his copybook, the menu for Friday's dinner. Hummus, spaghetti, salad, fruit. His mother would surely have some things on hand, so he wouldn't have to buy everything. For the salad and apples he would use the money his father had given him.

One good thing about your parents getting divorced—your father gives you money, trying to make it up to you!

Back to the menu. Hummus . . . that would take some doing. You had to boil the dried chickpeas and mash them and mix them with all that other stuff. And you had to put in just the right amounts, or it wouldn't be good. Toward the end, before his father left, Suhayl recalled, he'd complained vigorously about Mama's hummus—although he'd always liked it before.

At the break, as the students milled around in the small school yard and ate their snacks, Suhayl admired his friend Raeef's meat sandwich. Raeef always brought a good snack. His mother must be a good cook, Suhayl thought, and it gave him an idea.

"Would your mother tell me how to make hummus?"

"Make hummus? Why, what do you want to know for?"

"Well, I just thought . . ." *Should I tell him? Guess I'll have to.* "Well, you see, I'm going to make dinner for my mom."

Raeef doubled over, laughing. "You, cook dinner? You'll blow up the whole kitchen!"

"I will not! It's easy—anybody can cook. It's just that . . . you have to learn how, of course."

His friend got in a few more digs, which Suhayl bore patiently, but in the end Raeef agreed. "Okay, come home with me. She'll be there. She'll tell you how to make hummus. If you promise not to blow up our kitchen."

Sometimes it surprised Suhayl that of all the boys at school, he felt most friendly with Raeef, who was one of the few Christians. But so what? Raeef was fun to be with. He liked to laugh and tease, but he was never mean.

When they got to Raeef's building, Suhayl was surprised again. Raeef's family lived in a smaller flat than Suhayl's, and it was on the shabby side, with litter on the stairs and dirty paint. He'd always heard that Christian shopkeepers were rich. But as soon as Raeef's mother appeared, Suhayl found no more time for speculating. A large, loud woman with a face framed by frizzy red hair, she promptly bustled the boys into the kitchen and stuck pieces of raisin cake in their hands. When Raeef told her what Suhayl wanted, she burst into laughter.

"Well, dearie," she said at last, "the first thing you need is a good can opener. Get a couple of cans of chickpeas from the grocer. Your mama will have plenty of garlic—"

But Suhayl had already stopped listening. *Canned* chickpeas! He could still hear his father's voice, angry at his mother for making hummus from *canned* chickpeas. "No," he said, "I have to make it the other way, from dried ones."

Raeef's mother made a face. "But that's so much work, *habeebi,* all that soaking and cooking. Oh well, if that's what you want to do, then listen carefully."

After the hummus lesson, she shooed the boys into the sitting room, brought them a bowl of grapes and figs, and watched until they had settled down to their homework. Even after she had gone back to the kitchen, however, Suhayl felt eyes staring at him. He looked up. There were pictures on the wall, Christian pictures. Jesus the prophet and Maryam his mother and some other saint. They all gazed solemnly down at the two boys.

Suhayl knew the saints were supposed to look very holy, but to him they just looked tired. Like his mother. His mind strayed from the math problems. Raeef's family, he thought, seemed like happy people. Why did they want such gloomy pictures in their sitting room?

Would it make you a better person to have Jesus the prophet looking at you sadly, like you've failed at something important? Maybe I did fail. Maybe if I'd been a better person, Papa would have stayed.

But he knew it wasn't so. Jesus and Muhammad and all the prophets since Adam wouldn't have made any difference, once his father met that Huda lady. Suhayl let out an unguarded sigh.

Looking up from his paper, Raeef snickered. "What, is this baby stuff too hard for you?"

"No. Shut up." Focusing on his work again, Suhayl finished his problems carefully. He didn't want to give Jesus, or his mother, or even his teacher, any further reason to be disappointed in him. Besides, he hoped he could come again sometime to Raeef's house, because Raeef's mother was nice and gave them cake. He hoped her face always looked this cheery.

All week, Suhayl saved his money. It wasn't easy, not being able to buy chips and candy when everyone else did. But at the same time, keeping his plan in mind gave him a good feeling. For a couple of days Suhayl worried that Raeef might tell the other boys about his idea, but no one said anything. Raeef must have kept his promise.

After school on Friday he took a different bus, to the outdoor market. It was late in the day for shopping, but some vendors still had good vegetables. Suhayl bought lettuce, parsley, tomatoes, and onions, trying to look as though he really knew his way around. It wasn't all that hard to shop, he decided. He could probably do it again sometime.

As he wandered past the rows of vendors, looking for good apples, Suhayl noticed a couple of women completely covered in black. He stopped to stare at them. He'd seen such women before, although there weren't many who went to such extremes. But it was stupid, he thought, to have a piece of black cloth where a face should be. After all, God made people's faces and everything God did was good, so why cover your face like a shameful thing? That seemed a strange way to thank God for it.

Or were those women hiding, for some reason?

My mother wouldn't hide from the world, no matter how bad she might feel.

The thought jolted Suhayl back to his business. His mother—what if she came home early? He had to finish his shopping, hurry home, and start making dinner!

As soon as Suhayl reached the flat, he tossed his books on a table and got to work. Fortunately, he had remembered to soak the dried chickpeas the night before. The bowl was still hidden under his bed.

Cooking the chickpeas, however, was another matter. In no time at all, the pot boiled over. Yet although the chickpeas cooked and cooked, they never did become soft enough. Finally, tired of waiting, Suhayl poured out the hot water and started to work on them with a potato masher. Meanwhile, to speed things up he filled another saucepan with water, put in the spaghetti, and set it on the stove.

It wasn't easy, mashing those hard chickpeas. Suhayl was getting nervous, and the more he pounded, the more irritated he became.

Why should I have to do this, to make my mother happy? Why did somebody else make her unhappy? It's their fault. Bam, bam, bam! Take that, and that, and that, Papa! This'll take the smile off your face, Huda lady! POW!!

A sizzling sound distracted him. The spaghetti water was boiling over—even with the cover on tight! He'd forgotten about it, because he was so busy pounding.

No more time for those chickpeas. He added a good dollop of sesame-seed paste, some olive oil and lemon juice, and several big cloves of garlic that he'd chopped up. The hummus didn't look like any hummus Suhayl had ever seen. It looked awful. But it didn't taste too bad, if you liked garlic.

Now he'd have to deal with the spaghetti. It looked good and soft . . . maybe a little too soft. As he lifted it out with a big fork, the thick strands reminded him of the water weeds growing in the river that ran through Damascus. Like living things they slipped away from him, slithering here and there. At last he got most of the spaghetti scooped up and dumped into a bowl. Some grated cheese

SANTA CLAUS IN BAGHDAD AND OTHER STORIES

and chopped parsley would make it taste good, no matter what it looked like.

Fortunately, nothing could go wrong with the salad. Everything had to be washed, though, and somehow the kitchen floor got soaked.

When the salad was finished, Suhayl started to clean up the water and some spilled cheese. But glancing at the clock, he jumped. No time! He'd have to leave the pots and mixing spoons and bottles where they were, and dump all those bad pieces of lettuce into the garbage.

Oh, the table! Suhayl grabbed knives and forks and plates, and managed to get them on the table just as he heard his mother's key in the door. At the last instant, he dashed back to the kitchen, ripped off the apron he had tied around his neck, and tossed it onto the counter. Closing the kitchen door behind him, he took his stand by the entrance. He even managed to smile, hoping it would look natural.

"Why are you standing here, Suhayl?" his mother asked as she came in. "What's that smell?"

"Nothing! Everything's fine."

She had a plastic sack full of groceries. Suhayl lunged for it.

"Suhayl, don't be a nuisance," his mother said. "Let me get this out to the kitchen. It's heavy."

"No, no! I'll take it—you don't have to go in there." He seized the groceries, opened the kitchen door just enough to slip through, and a moment later rejoined his mother.

She looked irritated and worried. "Suhayl, what's wrong? What's going on in the kitchen?"

"Nothing. I told you, everything's fine."

"Come on, child, I'm too tired to deal with silliness."

"Well . . . well, Mama, what's happened is, you don't have to make dinner tonight. I've made it. Everything."

"Oh my God. I'd better see what you've done."

"No, it's fine! You're not supposed to do anything."

"Oh my God," she groaned again and headed for a chair in the sitting room.

Her feet hurt and she wanted to rest, that was plain. But the food was ready. The spaghetti was almost cold and beginning to look like a clod of green-speckled plastic. Suhayl grabbed his mother's hand and pulled her to the dining table. "You can rest after dinner," he said. "We have to eat now."

As Suhayl put the bowls of hummus, salad, and spaghetti in front of his mother, her eyes widened. She said nothing. Probably too tired, he thought. But as he looked closer at the lumpy hummus, the bloated spaghetti, and the bruised greens, he grew uneasy.

At last she spoke, in tones of disbelief. "Did you make all this?"

"Yes, every bit. I even cooked the chickpeas from scratch, the way Pa—the way you used to make hummus."

"Well, that's . . . wonderful, Suhayl! Let's see how it tastes."

As they ate, Suhayl told his mother about the hummus lesson and raisin cake at Raeef's house and then about his shopping. She listened and asked questions. And she ate some of everything.

"The salad is very good," she said. "Excellent. The spaghetti is tasty, just a tiny bit overcooked."

After a while they seemed to run out of talk. It looked to Suhayl as though his mother liked the dinner, but he couldn't quite tell. Watching her face closely, he saw little change of expression— and no smile.

When she was through, she stood up. "Suhayl, this was certainly delicious. Thank you, *habeebi*, thank you very much. Now I'd better get into the kitchen."

This time there was no way he could stop her. As she opened the door, he followed right behind, ready to explain. But when he now saw the kitchen as his mother must see it, his stomach tightened in dismay. Pools of boiled-over scum on the stove, the flooded floor, grated cheese and escaped spaghetti here and there, a puddle of oil where the bottle had tipped over, dishes and pots and pans piled high.

"Oh, Suhayl! It'll take me forever to clean up. . . ."

His mother's voice faded to a little squeak, and her mouth started to quiver. Panic gripped Suhayl.

It wasn't supposed to turn out like this—it should've been so easy! Did I fail again?

The sorrowful, disappointed face of Jesus the prophet popped into Suhayl's mind. He shut it out. No, he wasn't ready to accept reproof, not just yet. He pushed his mother out of the kitchen. To his relief she went without resisting, as if too battle-worn to do anything else, and dropped into the armchair in the sitting room.

"I'll clean it all up," he promised. "You don't have to do anything. And dinner's not even over yet. There's something more, so—so just rest there. Don't worry!"

Back to the horrible kitchen he went, put on water to boil for tea, and prepared the teapot. The loose tea spilled, but not too much. Then he arranged on a plate some sweets from the pastry shop, which had taken the very last of his money. He carried the dessert and a cup of hot tea, well sweetened, to his mother.

She drank the tea and ate two little cakes. As Suhayl sat on a low hassock near her feet, watching, he could see her start to relax a little.

At last she spoke. "Why did you want to make this nice dinner for us, Suhayl? To—to experiment, or just to have something to do after school? I could have shown you how—"

"No, Mama, no!"

"Then why—"

"I did it so you could rest when you got home from work and be happy for a while. I'm sorry I made the kitchen so messy."

His mother did not answer right away. She just stared down at the small paper napkin in her lap with cake crumbs on it, and her mouth looked as though she'd eaten something bitter. Suhayl was afraid she would scold him . . . and he couldn't really blame her. The kitchen was such a sight.

But as he gazed at her face, lined and coarsened and sad, he suddenly felt overwhelmed. *Is this really my mother? It can't be! Somebody else has taken her place, somebody I don't even know.* The thought nearly broke his heart.

Finally she spoke, and even sitting close, he had to listen intently to her low voice. "I will always remember, Suhayl," she said, "how you made a wonderful dinner for me. And how happy I've been to have you all these years."

Had he heard right? Yes, she was looking at him, and although her eyes were reddened, she was smiling. It was a curiously shy smile, shy and trembling. But it was a smile at last—and he knew he could believe it.

"I'll remember, too, Mama," said Suhayl. "And I'll always remember how beautiful you are." He inched the hassock closer so that he could lean toward her. As she put her arm around him, he rested his face against her knee. He was too old, he knew, to do such a childish thing . . . but there would probably never be another chance.

3

The Hand of Fatima

A STORY FROM LEBANON

Aneesi paused outside the dining room. She had spent the long, hot summer morning helping Sitt Zeina prepare a lavish lunch, had waited on the guests without a single slip, and had just finished clearing the dessert dishes. She was tired and hungry, and her plastic sandals chafed from so much running back and forth. All she wanted right now was to sit down in the kitchen and enjoy the leftovers.

But something had caught her attention. Holding the silver serving plates still half full of pastries, she lingered in the hallway to listen.

Sitt Zeina was telling her husband, in no uncertain terms, "We *must* have that garden wall repaired, Yusuf. You know, where the old fig tree is pushing it over. You've put it off long enough, and costs are going up every day. Besides, there's a lot more we should do with the garden."

Before Dr. Jubeili could answer, one of the guests broke in with a laugh. "What are you thinking of, Zeina? Big ideas for the Jubeili estate?"

"Oh, nothing too extravagant," she answered. "Just terraces for my roses, with good walls of well-fitted stones. There aren't many fine old villas like ours left close to Beirut—what with those dreadful apartment buildings springing up everywhere. We must make the most of this one."

Aneesi could hear Dr. Jubeili sigh. "Zeina, have you any idea what workers are getting paid these days? Stonemasons can charge whatever they want. Lebanese ones, that is. Syrian workers are cheaper—but just try to find one who knows how to do good stonework."

A charge of excitement ran through Aneesi. *I know one,* she thought—*my father!*

A few days earlier, a letter had arrived from her older brother Hussein, who was at home in Syria. Papa needed more work, Hussein wrote. He had to borrow continually, just to feed the six people who depended on him. Hussein was thinking of quitting school so he could get a job.

No, he mustn't! Aneesi was dismayed at the thought. After all, she had left school at twelve so that Hussein, being a boy and smart, could go on with his education. For two years she'd been sending home every bit of her earnings—and now Hussein was saying that her money and Papa's miserable pay still weren't enough.

But there must be another solution. Maybe, Hussein wrote, their father could find work in Lebanon, where a few weeks' pay would feed a family for months in a Syrian village. What were the chances of Papa finding something in the town where Aneesi was living?

Aneesi had delayed her answer to Hussein, afraid that her father didn't stand much chance of finding work in Lebanon. Many Syrian laborers, most of them young, strong men, came to Lebanon for manual day-by-day jobs. Competition was keen, and Papa was not as hardy as he had been. But he had something in his favor, at least: his skill as a stonemason.

And now, out of the blue, the Jubeilis were talking about hiring somebody to do stonework. What luck!

For a moment Aneesi recalled Sitt Zeina speaking to her—more than once, in fact—about not listening to the family's private conversations. It was an improper, low kind of behavior to "eavesdrop," as Sitt Zeina had put it. Aneesi had bristled inwardly at being admonished, but at least it was better than being thought of as too dull to care what people were saying, like a pet dog. Besides, Aneesi found it hard to resist listening. With no family or friends of her own, what else could she do but share, in a second-hand way, the Jubeilis' family life? So now she'd eavesdropped again—but maybe this time Sitt Zeina would be glad of it.

Although almost too excited to eat, Aneesi soon felt hunger pangs again and settled down to a plate of leftovers. She was chewing the last piece of broiled chicken when Sitt Zeina came into the kitchen to prepare coffee. Swallowing quickly, Aneesi spoke up with uncustomary boldness. "Sitt Zeina, I couldn't help hearing something—I didn't mean to, but I was just leaving the dining room—"

"Yes? What is it, Aneesi? As you can see, I'm busy."

"Well . . . are you going to mend the wall by the driveway?"

With raised eyebrows Sitt Zeina shot a disapproving look at Aneesi. Sitt Zeina was a tall, handsome woman with thick black hair worn loose to her shoulders. It made her look very young, except for the lines in her face that deepened when she took on serious matters. But rather than another lecture about proper behavior, she gave a dramatic sigh. "So you heard what we were saying about that wall. Why does it concern you?"

"Because, Sitt Zeina, because I—I know a good worker you could hire."

"Really?"

"Yes. My father."

"But he's working in Syria."

"He could come, Sitt Zeina. He has done stonework, a lot of it, and he is very good. He learned from his father, who built our house. He built a wall all around the government building in the village—a nice wall, with places for flowers. He knows how to cut stone carefully and trim the pieces to fit, and everybody says he can be trusted to do his best."

Considering this news, Sitt Zeina frowned in thought. "I thought he had a different kind of job," she said.

"Yes, he drives a car for the government, but they don't pay much. If he comes here to work, they won't mind, I think, and will let him have the same job when he goes back. He is honest and good—you can count on him. And . . ." Aneesi paused, uncertain.

"And what?"

"He would not take very much. I mean, you would not have to pay him as much as a Lebanese worker."

"Hmmm." Sitt Zeina reached into the cupboard for the small coffee cups, then started heating finely ground coffee and water in a small pot. "Well, I don't know. I'll take it up with my husband."

As Aneesi went back to her work, washing the dishes and putting the kitchen in order, she tried to force herself to relax. She had done what she could, but hopes and doubts kept pricking at her. If only Dr. Jubeili would agree to hire her father, it would help the family so much! Hussein could stay in school—and she could be a daughter again for a while. Two weeks a year, all that her contract allowed, was such a tiny bit of time to spend with her family, to be a daughter. The rest of the year she was just a maid.

Just a maid. Even now Aneesi sometimes shuddered as she thought of the risk she'd taken in leaving home. Her parents had not wanted her to go, and there had been tearful, noisy scenes. In the end, though, the thought of the money she could earn outweighed their fears—and of course the agency had assured them she would be treated well. Just the same, how naïve and trusting she'd been! She could so easily have been hired by a family who would have overworked her and crushed her spirit. But God had been merciful and had sent her to the Jubeili home. Once again, Aneesi gave thanks.

The next morning, Sitt Zeina had news for Aneesi. Dr. Jubeili had agreed to give her father a chance. "We've been pleased with your work, Aneesi," she added, "and we know life is hard for your family. We hope this arrangement will work out well for all of us."

"Yes, of course!" Aneesi answered. "Thank you, Sitt Zeina. I think you will be satisfied." She wanted to skip, jump, and shout with happiness, but she kept her feet in place and her manner composed. A good maid knew how to behave.

In any case, she had enough work to keep her from thinking too much about her father coming. Maya Jubeili soon reminded her of that. Maya was seventeen, romping through the summer before her last year of secondary school. She came and went in the house so quickly that she barely took time for anything except to tell Aneesi what to do next.

Now, in her usual manner, Maya came dashing into the kitchen, gave her mother a quick kiss on the cheek, then turned to Aneesi. "Wash my good black jeans today, Aneesi, will you? And anything else you find loose in my room. I want to wear the jeans tonight and they'll need to be ironed, so you'd better get busy. Oh, and do a better job ironing, Aneesi. There were wrinkles on the front of my pink silk blouse."

Aneesi managed to keep calm as she answered politely. "That blouse gets wrinkles from hanging in the closet, Sitt Maya."

"Well, whatever. Do something about it. I have to look nice, not like some old beggar woman." Maya whirled out of the kitchen and out of the house, off to meet friends at a café. Sitt Zeina shook her head but said nothing.

Aneesi left her work in the kitchen and went to Maya's room, where she collected the clothes draped on chairs and dropped in corners. Standing before the mirror, she held the black jeans up to her body for a moment, trying to imagine what she would look like in them. No, it wasn't even worth dreaming about. Maya's jeans fit like a second skin . . . a girl had to be slim as an eel to wear them. Aneesi's own stocky shape was doomed to baggy slacks.

The sound of voices from the direction of the front door startled her. Maya was back for some reason, talking excitedly with her mother. A moment later she hurtled into the bedroom, closely followed by Sitt Zeina. Seeing the black jeans still in Aneesi's hands, she seized them.

"Here, I have to—" Maya jammed a hand into one pocket and then into the other. A smile of relief flashed over her face as she withdrew her hand and tossed the jeans back at Aneesi. "I've got them, Mama, everything's okay!"

"Really, Maya!" Sitt Zeina started to chide her but was too late. Maya, stuffing something in her purse, was already dashing out of the bedroom.

"That girl!" said Sitt Zeina, as the front door slammed shut once more. "She is so careless these days. So much money, just forgotten in her pocket!" Frowning in annoyance, she, too, left the room, her dignified steps a contrast with Maya's headlong rush. Aneesi let out her breath in relief.

As she went on with her morning's work, Aneesi allowed her thoughts to run ahead to those happy days when she and Papa would be together and he could do work that he enjoyed and took pride in, while earning good money. Oh, how lucky it was that she had eavesdropped on the Jubeilis' lunchtime conversation!

Then came a break that Aneesi looked forward to: her lesson with Iskandar, a few afternoons a week. She often wondered how Maya and her brother could be so different. Iskandar, serious and conscientious, was studying education at the American University of Beirut. Finding Aneesi intelligent, he had decided not only to help her with Arabic but to teach her some English.

Today Iskandar greeted her with a chuckle. "I hear my sister left a treasure in her jeans pocket for you to put through the wash."

"She found it, thanks to God," said Aneesi.

"That Maya . . . she's got her head in the clouds these days, and she thinks money grows in the garden, but she'll get better. Now, let's work."

After a while Iskandar put down the book they were reading together and sat back. "That's very good, Aneesi. You've got a quick mind. You shouldn't have to be a maid forever. I've been thinking. . . . Know what you should do?"

She looked at him, hoping, and waited to hear more.

"Take a commercial course at the YWCA in Beirut, in a couple of years. Then you could get a real job. I mean—" Iskandar corrected himself—"this is a good job for you now, and you're a real help to Mama. But if you learn some office skills, then you can start to earn a lot more."

Aneesi smiled, quietly delighted. At last! This was the sort of thing she'd been hoping to hear. A job in an office someday, maybe as a secretary or even a manager, an important job with a good salary—the realization of her dreams. It was with this dream that she had left her family: to help them out and to gain a better life for herself.

Just the same, she feigned a modest response to Iskandar. "Really, do you think I could? Oh yes, I'd like that. Thank you, Mr. Iskandar." She could hardly wait to tell her father what Mr. Iskandar had said. Papa would be so proud.

After a day's ride from Syria in a battered old taxi, Aneesi's father arrived, tired and rumpled. Aneesi was thrilled to see him—and in the next instant, worried. He had grown so thin in the nine or ten months since she'd last been home. Was he really healthy?

Anyway, she knew he would eat well here. The Jubeilis believed in good food and plenty of it, and they were generous to the people who worked for them. Papa could sleep in the space at the rear of the house where the garden tools were kept—Iskandar had helped Aneesi move things around to make room.

As soon as they were alone, on the terrace outside the tool room, Aneesi's father hugged her again. A feeling both happy and sad went through her as she smelled the familiar old Papa-smell of tobacco and garlic, the mothballs in which his suit was kept, and the faint overlay of soap. Then he stepped back to look at her. His weathered face took on a look of eager happiness, which had been hidden during the polite greetings with his new employers.

"Aneesi, I have news for you. Good news!"

Something about Hussein—he must have passed his exams with high scores! Aneesi smiled, eager to hear.

"I am so glad to tell you, daughter," her father went on. "There is a man from the village—a very good man—who has asked for you." He waited to see her reaction.

Aneesi's heart suddenly went cold. Her smile faded, and she sat down slowly on a white plastic chair by the door, unable to meet his eyes.

"Papa . . ."

He continued in a lower voice. "Listen, my daughter. Let me tell you about him. He is the son of the postmaster. They are a good family, respected by everybody. Fareed is not too old—I think around thirty—and he has not been married before. He is educated, and he has a store in Safita, only half an hour from the village. Electrical things, a good business. He is kind and good-hearted, and not bad-looking."

Aneesi heard the words, but they meant nothing to her. After a moment she asked, "Why does he want me, Papa? Why doesn't he marry a nice woman in Safita?"

"He wants a girl from the village, my daughter. That is important to him. He does not have a cousin whom he wants to marry. And he knows our family. We are not well-off, but we are good people. He knows you are a good girl. And . . ."

Aneesi's father paused to look around for something to sit on, then lowered himself onto a pile of firewood that lay alongside the wall. "He knows you are smart. The teacher told him you were one of the best students he ever had. Yes, that teacher still talks about you."

A tiny flicker of warmth quickened in Aneesi as she recalled the teacher. He had been angry with her father for letting her leave school. Twice he had come to the house, and the two men had argued in loud voices. Hearing them, Aneesi had felt torn and had almost changed her mind. But it had been her own decision, after all, to work in Lebanon, her decision to help the family—and herself—in this way.

Now Aneesi looked up at her father, her eyes starting to fill with tears. "I am learning English, Papa. Mr. Iskandar is teaching me. He says I should—"

"That's good, daughter. Fareed Fakhoury will like that. He doesn't want a wife who can do nothing but cook."

"Papa, I'm not even fifteen yet!"

He made calming gestures with his large-knuckled hands. "Mr. Fareed is willing to wait, until you are sixteen or so. He knows you have to grow up a bit more."

The happiness had gone from her father's face, and it cut Aneesi to the heart to see the anxious look return to his eyes. If only it had been good news about Hussein that he brought, how she would have rejoiced with him! But for two years now she had been on her own, learning and growing. She was no longer a child who had to accept everything decided for her. Surely that meant something—surely her father could see she had changed.

"Papa," she said, rubbing at her moist cheek, "I don't want to marry. Mr. Fareed may be a very good man, and I know you would not want me to marry somebody who wasn't. But I don't want it."

"Daughter, this is your chance! Any girl would envy you. And your family will benefit . . . you have to think of that, too, you know."

Another thought came to Aneesi, shading her voice with bitterness. "And you wouldn't have to worry about me any longer, would you?" What she meant was "my virtue," but she could not bring herself to say it.

Now it was her father's turn to harden. "My daughter, I cannot force you to marry a man you don't want. That is against the law, and it is not my way. But I require that you meet Fareed Fakhoury and decide after you have had a chance to get to know him. You will see, my daughter, that you would be stupid not to accept."

"Yes, Papa," whispered Aneesi, her heart heavy. She left him and returned to her work in the kitchen.

But her mind was turbulent. She thought back to her first weeks in this new country, how hard it had been to learn new ways, to live with a different family . . . how baffling to bump into unfamiliar ideas and assumptions . . . how humiliating to make mistakes and blunders time after time. She had cried quietly so often at night in her bed, missing her home, where everything was simple and familiar. All that unhappiness, and everything she had learned since then—did it all count for nothing? Would she have to give up her hopes?

For most of July, Aneesi's father worked on the Jubeilis' garden walls. Dr. Jubeili hired a second worker, a muscular young man who could do most of the heavy lifting, and the two men made a good team. Madame Jubeili was so pleased with the walls that she made more and more elaborate plans for the terraces and rose gardens.

It made Aneesi happy to see her father content in his work. He looked healthier, and the lines of anxiety eased in his face. As the days passed and he said nothing more about the man who had "asked for her," Aneesi hoped that he had decided not to pursue the matter.

Then, as if to make life even better, Maya Jubeili went away to visit friends at a fashionable seaside resort. For a week, Aneesi would not have to worry about the constant demands and prodding, let alone the clothes strewn everywhere around the house.

One evening soon after Maya's departure, Aneesi's father came to her in the kitchen, his face crinkled in a happy smile.

"Mr. Iskandar took me with him to Beirut this afternoon, my daughter, and I bought something for you. Hold out your hand."

Sweets? Or a fancy headband to control her curly hair? No, what Aneesi found in her palm, in a small plastic box, was a charm of gold, shaped like a hand with a turquoise in the center.

"The Hand of Fatima," said her father. "Not very big, but it will bring you good luck. It will protect you. Someday you will have much more gold—but this is a start."

61

"Papa . . . Papa, thank you!" For a moment Aneesi didn't know what more to say. She had never owned gold before, not even a tiny piece. Gold meant something that could always be counted on, especially for a woman. Then the inevitable question had to come out. "But . . . Papa, how could you pay for it? Something like this costs a lot."

"Yes, I know. But don't worry. Dr. Jubeili gave me my first pay today, and I wanted to do something nice for you. It is not so much. I am saving the rest of my pay, you can be sure."

Aneesi kissed him and went right to her little room next to the kitchen, where she tucked the gold charm into a safe place. But her heart was not completely happy. Could Papa really afford to buy gold for her? Wasn't it an extravagance? Or worse—a chill went through her—could it be a sort of bribe, to encourage her to look with favor on Mr. Fareed Fakhoury? Aneesi tried to bury that thought, but it lingered.

A few days later, Maya came home from the seaside resort, sun-tanned, beautiful, and sulky. In the late afternoon she sat with her mother on the balcony, while Aneesi served them lemonade. A strange nervousness seemed to underlie Maya's casual pose, and Aneesi wondered whether anything had gone wrong during the visit.

"Did you get to all the boutiques, dear?" asked Sitt Zeina. "Silly question. Well, show me what you bought. What were the shoes like? Did you find a nice purse for your cousin's wedding?"

Maya appeared to examine her manicure. Then she said, bluntly, "No."

"Well, what happened? Didn't the stores have nice things?"

No answer came from Maya, who ordinarily would have given a complete inventory of every boutique she visited. Aneesi could feel Maya's gaze on her, but she kept busy setting down the glasses of lemonade, the sugar, napkins, and sweet biscuits. Curious about this unusual behavior, she wanted to hear more.

Finally Maya said, "I didn't have enough money."

Sitt Zeina sat up straight. "Enough money? Of course you did! I know prices are high there, but I gave you two hundred-thousand-pound notes just before you left. That certainly should have been enough for a decent pair of shoes and a purse. Now, what happened?"

"I don't know, Mama. All I remember is . . ." Maya paused again.

There was no way Aneesi could stall any longer. She left the balcony but paused inside the sitting room, where she could still hear the conversation.

"*What*, Maya?"

"Well . . . this is what happened." Maya's voice dropped, and Aneesi strained to listen. "You gave me the money just before I left, remember? And Iskandar was waiting in the car and already getting impatient and honking the horn. And he knows it always rattles me when he does that—I hate it! So it wasn't my fault I got nervous, was it? And then I remembered I'd forgotten my cell phone, so I had to go back for it. But I didn't want to drag along my purse and that big box of sweets you made me take, so I set them down on the garden wall for just a minute, while—" Maya broke off the story.

A moment later Aneesi heard Sitt Zeina call to her. "Aneesi! You have plenty to do in the kitchen. We'll call you if we need you."

So Aneesi heard no more, but what she had heard disquieted her. And that evening she knew that Dr. and Madame Jubeili were talking to her father, with Maya and Iskandar present. Aneesi had been told to stay in her room.

The next morning, everything happened so fast she could hardly grasp what was going on. Just the day before, she had been so happy to see her father working contentedly, pruning the old fig tree, repairing the wall for the rose garden. Now he was here in the kitchen with her, distraught. Worse, he was not wearing his work clothes but the shabby suit and frayed white shirt he'd had on when he first arrived.

He spoke briefly, in a subdued, hoarse voice. Aneesi could sense the effort with which he controlled himself.

"They are sending me away, my daughter. They say I stole. They think I took money from Sitt Maya's purse when she left it on the wall. I remember when it happened. I was working near there, and the boy was working in back of the house. I saw the purse. Of course I did not touch it. But Sitt Maya could not find the money when she looked in her purse, so they think I took it. And now they don't want me any more."

At that point Iskandar came out to the kitchen. Looking pained, he spoke curtly. "Sorry, we've got to hurry or you'll miss the bus to Damascus."

Unable to utter a word, Aneesi kissed her father good-bye. As soon as he had left, she sat down at the kitchen table and wept.

She tried to keep the little Hand of Fatima out of her thoughts, but stealthily it worked its way in. When had Papa bought it? Yes, just a day or two after Sitt Maya had gone away. Could he really . . . ? No, never! Impossible! Still . . . With sudden passion, Aneesi hated the Hand of Fatima. And she hated herself more, for allowing such hateful thoughts into her head.

In the next day or two, no one said anything out of the ordinary to Aneesi. She went about her work as always, but unsmiling, with downcast eyes. She took pains to avoid even the smallest slip and said nothing except when spoken to. Maya avoided her, and Mr. Iskandar said he was too busy for lessons.

On the third day, Aneesi went to Maya's room to gather up the clothes for laundering. As she did so, an image slipped into her mind . . . the black jeans, money in the pocket, a few weeks back. And with that image came an impelling thought. What had Maya been wearing on her drive to the resort? Aneesi didn't know; she hadn't seen Maya leave. But her sudden, desperate hunch held the only possible hope.

In an increasing frenzy, she searched through all the jeans and shorts. Nothing. She found a jacket and a couple of shirts with pockets lying around the room. Nothing. Then she glanced at the open closet—but no, she couldn't search there. Clothes hanging in the closet were private. She looked behind chairs, under the bed. No clothes hiding there.

Finally Aneesi gave up in despair. Her eyes blurring with tears of frustration, she tried to get on with her work. She gathered up an armful of clothes and was about to carry them to the washing machine when she noticed something on the closet floor. A garment must have fallen from a hanger. Setting down her armload, Aneesi picked it up . . . a light cardigan sweater. Could Maya have been wearing that recently? Sometimes, even in midsummer, morning fog made the air cool.

In fumbling haste, Aneesi examined the sweater. Her heart suddenly seemed to pound as she found a small pocket. She stuck her fingers in—and they touched folded paper. Trembling, she drew it out. Two bank notes, two hundred thousand pounds.

For a minute or two, unable to take the next step, Aneesi sat on the edge of Maya's bed. Then she left the room to look for Sitt Zeina.

Elegantly dressed and ready to go down to Beirut, Sitt Zeina was checking her appearance at a mirror in the front hall. She turned with a frown of irritation. "What is it, girl? Can't you see, I'm—"

Still half in a daze, Aneesi held out the money and the cardigan sweater.

Sitt Zeina stared blankly at the bills. Then, backing up to a chair, she sat down heavily. "Oh, my God," she whispered. "The money was in Maya's pocket all the time. That careless girl, so careless with money . . . she took off the sweater and forgot all about it. And we accused the poor man. Oh, God forgive us."

That evening the family gathered again in the sitting room. After a while, Aneesi was asked to join them. Maya sat with slumped shoulders, streaks of black mascara on her cheeks.

"I'm sorry, Aneesi," she mumbled. "I was in such a hurry. . . . I didn't know what I was doing. I thought . . ."

"No, you didn't think!" growled her brother. "And you didn't know what you were doing. You never do, these days."

Sitt Zeina gave them both a warning look, then turned to Aneesi. "We are so very sorry, Aneesi," she said in a low voice. "We hope you and your father will forgive us."

Though at a loss for words, Aneesi lifted her head and tried to look Sitt Zeina in the eye. She nodded slightly.

With a cough, Sitt Zeina spoke more diffidently. "We appreciated his good work. He is a fine workman. Do . . . do you think he would come back?"

Dr. Jubeili broke in sharply. "Of course not! What do you think? The man has his pride."

Aneesi could tell that the gruff voice covered his own regret and embarrassment. And she knew he was absolutely right.

But her own feelings were so mixed up she wondered how she could ever see her life clearly again. Now, remembering how she had yielded to even faint suspicions about her father, *she* felt like the betrayer. And no matter how unfair it was, she felt responsible. She had brought him here, to the place where he was forced to suffer such a harsh blow. It would have been better, she thought, if she had never overheard that conversation about stone walls. Now there was only one thing she could do.

"I must go to my father," she said.

As soon as she could pack her things, Aneesi left the Jubeili home. Dr. Jubeili gave her the remaining pay for the days her father had worked, plus a large bonus. Aneesi was sure her father would accept it, pride or no pride.

Sitt Zeina said quietly, "You could come back, Aneesi, maybe later on, when you're ready." Aneesi thanked her and said nothing more.

Iskandar drove Aneesi to a nearby town where she could get the weekly taxi to Syria. Neither spoke on the way, but when they arrived and he had taken her suitcase from the car, he looked at her with concern. "Aneesi, I have a couple of books for you, an English grammar and a book of short stories I think you'll like. Remember what I told you, Aneesi. You can do good things in life, important things. And . . . come back, if you possibly can."

"Thank you, I will," she said, aware that her answer would serve for everything he'd said. Then she climbed into the battered old taxi, and it got under way.

After a while Aneesi took the gold charm from her small purse, placed it on her palm, and studied it. What did it mean, the Hand of Fatima? Luck . . . protection? A token of her father's love, surely. But also, she feared, a claim for obedience.

67

No, it meant more—it must! The Hand of Fatima also stood for strength, power.

For the first time in days, Aneesi felt her heart quickening, her thoughts becoming coherent. She was headed, she knew, for the most difficult encounter of her young life: facing her father—and what he wanted for her. But even though she would probably stand alone, she would stand firm. The Hand would help her . . . a reminder that her fate must rest in her own hands.

Aneesi closed her fingers around the gold trinket. Then she turned to gaze out the grimy window of the taxi, as it hurtled on through stony hills scattered with fig trees, pines, and raw new buildings.

4

The Olive Grove

A STORY FROM PALESTINE

Hustling along behind the other boys, Mujahhid stooped to grab a stone, then quickly caught up. About halfway across the open square they stopped. Right next to the military checkpoint was a two-story stone house that the Israelis had taken over. The boys could see the olive-drab helmets of soldiers behind sandbags on the flat rooftop.

"Take that, you dogs!" Mujahhid shouted in Arabic, hurling the stone toward them. "Get out of Bethlehem—it's *our* town!"

Shouting with every throw, he then flung whatever he could get his hands on . . . chunks of plaster, pebbles, concrete rubble, worn bricks from the older streets. The soldiers, of course, had every other kind of missile—bullets, stun grenades, tear gas, shells. Today they weren't firing, though, not yet. The boys grew bolder and started making dashes to throw from closer range.

You can get near enough to see faces, thought Mujahhid, *but not what's in their eyes. Anyway, they're all the same . . . they all hate us. Even the young guys, just three or four years older than us, hard as their rifles.*

In a brief lull, Mujahhid heard shattered glass fall to the street with a strangely musical jingle. Then the sound of yelling again filled his ears, some of the boys' voices hoarse and loud, others so high they seemed—like the tinkling glass—to belong to a different time and place, like children playing in a school yard. For a moment Mujahhid felt as though he and the others were playing, too, in the warm November sun.

He looked around for Nawar, his best friend. "Come on, Nawar! I can throw twice as far as you!"

In answer, Nawar grabbed a large chunk of plaster and, with a grunt, hurled it in the direction of the soldiers. Falling short, it smashed to bits. Mujahhid laughed and Nawar whirled on him, then broke into a sheepish grin.

"Okay," Nawar said, "we'll see who's stronger. We both throw together—*now*!"

Two stones went hurtling toward their target, but Mujahhid's went astray and hit a battered Dumpster. He was just about to let fly another when, above the shouting, he heard the first notes of the call to prayer from a mosque close by. Pausing, he let his arm drop and retreated a few steps. His parents had raised him to take prayer seriously, and his instinctive response was to welcome the call as a moment of peace.

But as he listened to the rise and fall of the chant and the familiar, beautiful words, Mujahhid felt as though a wound in his heart had been torn open afresh. It was near that mosque that his older brother had been shot just a month ago. Killed on his way to prayer—as if he was being denied his right to pray, denied his religion! He'd been given the funeral of a martyr, even though he wasn't a fighter.

The sounds and sights of that day came back to Mujahhid . . . the call from the mosque sounding so sad, and all the church bells in Bethlehem ringing and ringing. Many hundreds of people had stood quietly and listened in mourning, Muslims and Christians together. They were all one in the struggle, Muslims and Christians, all one people. Remembering, Mujahhid's heart felt full of terrible grief . . . and a strange kind of triumph.

Now, for the sake of his brother, his people, his religion, he fought every chance he could. Surely that was what God wanted him to do—help resist the army that had oppressed them for thirty-three years now, so that Israel could gradually take over more and more of the Palestinians' land. Surely God wanted the Palestinian people to be free in their own country. Then someday, everybody—Muslims and Christians and Jews—could get together and work things out fairly.

A new wave of exhilaration gripped Mujahhid. He was helping to bring that day—he was part of the struggle for a better future! After all, hadn't his parents named him Mujahhid, the one who struggles for a good cause? This struggle was the most important jihad he could ever hope to fight, a sacred duty to fight for his own homeland. With a yell, he hurled another large stone.

A few of the boys had started to throw Molotov cocktails. The homemade missiles flew toward the army post, but the flames went out in midair. Smashing on the littered street, the bottles added the smell of kerosene to the stench of tear gas drifting over from a few streets away.

Just then, Mujahhid heard an ominous rumble. Tanks? Yes! From the far side of the army post came a couple of tanks, grinding their way toward the boys. The sight and the sound filled Mujahhid with cold fear. It always did, no matter how many days he'd been out in the streets.

"Come on—the next street!" yelled Nawar, yanking at Mujahhid's shirt sleeve. With the other boys they raced back through the broad square, turned and tore down an alley. Reaching another open area, they found a couple of soldiers in a jeep and started pelting the vehicle. The soldiers yelled and gunned the motor but didn't come after them.

Suddenly Nawar jerked upright in a little jump. Then, with a sigh, he crumpled onto the rough pavement. Mujahhid and the others turned, baffled. What was wrong with him? They'd heard nothing. But already blood, from his neck or chest, was seeping into the dust. He lay still, not even a tremor.

One of the older boys let out a hoarse cry. "A sniper—with a silencer! We've got to get out of here!"

Terrified, Mujahhid started to run, looking for a sheltering doorway or another alley. A chip flew off a limestone wall nearby, then another. The sniper was still shooting. Mujahhid wanted to run forever, anywhere to get away from bullets and tanks and grenades.

But—Nawar! . . .

He dashed back to his friend, grabbed an arm, and managed to pull Nawar over to one side of the street. For a moment he thought he heard Nawar speak, and he bent down to look into his friend's face. With a sickening spasm in his stomach, he realized there was no life in those wide-open eyes.

The stone houses on this street were old, their walls rising right at the edge of the paving and their windows tightly shuttered. Would anyone help? Cold with panic, Mujahhid looked around.

Then he heard a woman's voice. "Here—bring him in here!" Twisting his head as he tried to get a better grip on Nawar's limp body, he saw a door open a crack.

Mujahhid dragged Nawar a few meters to the door, over a worn stone threshold, and into a dark hallway. Although he looked as small as a child, Nawar felt heavy. Mujahhid gently let his friend down as the woman hovered nearby, muttering a mixture of curses and prayers in Arabic. Was she young or old? In the darkness he couldn't tell. Then Mujahhid felt a strong pair of hands pull him away. Dazed, he let himself be pushed through the shadowy first-floor rooms of the house.

"We'll get help—*yallah,* go home." A man's voice. "Go out the back way, I don't think anybody's on that side. Where d'you live?"

Mujahhid told him the street. He barely knew what he was saying and his teeth chattered with shock, but the man understood him.

"Good, not far. Keep low and run like hell. You kids, damn fools, throwing stones at an army—!"

Mujahhid squeezed out a half-opened door and heard it click shut behind him. Heart pounding, he raced up one narrow street and down another, keeping close to walls, expecting any instant to be dropped by an unheard bullet. Soon he reached familiar territory, then his apartment building, and home. His mother, seeing Nawar's blood all over his shirt, welcomed him with screams of horror.

Everyone in the neighborhood soon knew of Nawar's death, and how he'd been struck . . . the silent snipers gave people a double chill of fear. However dreadful the roar of tanks and helicopter gunships, even more terrifying was the knowledge that death could strike without a sound.

Her gray hair loose and tousled, clothes in disarray, Mujahhid's mother wept all evening. His father silently paced the length of the small apartment, smoking one cigarette after another, down to the butt. Mujahhid sat on the bed in his room, listening to his mother moan his brother's name over and over. Again he heard in his mind the rhythm of the church bells, mingling with the call from the mosque. And it seemed, too, he could still hear the odd little sigh that Nawar had let out as he fell.

He remembered, too, how his mother had wailed when the Israelis shut the schools again, a couple of weeks back. Fearing that nothing would keep him off the streets now, she and Papa had yelled at him, reasoned, argued, threatened. They'd even locked him in the tiny bedroom that he now had all to himself . . . but he'd managed to get out the window easily enough. Well, something was really going to change for him now. He knew he had it coming.

In the morning Mujahhid's parents directed him to the couch in the sitting room. His mother had pulled herself together, and the black blouse and skirt she wore in mourning were once more tidy. Mujahhid sat with hunched shoulders and prepared himself for a lecture.

"No more," said his father gruffly. "We can't trust you. You're going to stay with my sister. You're going to Beit al-Makhfiya."

"What?" Thunderstruck, Mujahhid stared. "I have to go stay with my aunt? In that miserable little village? When? How long?"

"As long as it takes. You go tomorrow. We've already arranged for a car."

Mujahhid's dismay boiled over. "I don't want to go! I belong here—with the other fighters! And—and to help you, help in Papa's shop. You need me here!"

Mujahhid's mother exploded. "We need you *here*—to worry about you day and night? To wonder when somebody will come tell us *you've* been shot, too? We need that? May God save us! We need to know you're alive! You're the only child we have left, Mujahhid."

"*Ummi*—Mama, listen—!"

"You listen. *Ibni*, my son, we support the resistance—you know that. But we've given enough of our family. It's bad enough to suffer what we have to under *them*, without losing *both* sons in the fight. You're going to stay with your aunt, out of trouble."

"But, Mama, if we keep up the jihad, we won't have to suffer forever—"

"Jihad! Don't talk to me about that. Look, Mujahhid *habibi*, go to the mosque to be close to God. Try to understand what He wants of you. But don't listen to talk of jihad!"

Mujahhid glared at her. What did she know? She was just a worker in a textile factory, and his father a sandwich-shop owner. He tried again.

"I have to go on with the struggle—"

She made a sharp gesture, cutting him off. "*Khallas!* Finished! Go to your room and get your books together—you're going to study there, by God. I'll get your clothes ready. The car leaves at seven in the morning, and it may take all day to get there."

Mujahhid pulled himself up from the sagging couch and, at his father's nod of dismissal, headed for his room. *All day?* he thought. *All day to go the twenty kilometers to that nowhere village? What do I have to do—push the car, with the other passengers on my back?* He was glad to have thought of something even slightly funny— it helped him walk away with a scrap of pride. Then, behind the closed door of his room, he let resentment snarl within him.

So this was what became of the great resistance fighter. He got packed off to a tiny village to live with his aunt and his girl-cousin and his grandmother. A house of women. He got stuck out there, away from Bethlehem—his home, his friends, the holy sites. Away from the action, where he was needed. The shame of it! Why should he be safe and sound while his friends were going on with the struggle, fighting for the freedom of their people?

He heard his mother in the kitchen heating water to scrub his clothes, and he knew that one of those garments would be the shirt stained with Nawar's blood. The image of Nawar lying crumpled on the street, his arms so thin, came back to Mujahhid. He remembered how his first instinct had been to run, and again he felt a searing shame. At the same time, another thought hit him, like a stone. He had seen death before, sure . . . he'd wept over his own brother's body. But Nawar—that was the first time he'd seen a close friend go down, so suddenly, so unexpectedly. Mujahhid remembered looking into the unseeing eyes of his friend.

What would it be like to suffer pain, to live the rest of his life a cripple, blind, or paralyzed—or dead, for that matter? Too horrible even to think about! Yes, he felt almost relieved not to face that danger anymore.

Immediately he caught himself. Relieved to give up, to betray the jihad? I *am* a coward, thought Mujahhid.

As they waited for the taxi, his mother had hugged and kissed him until he'd felt steamy with embarrassment. But he'd let her, and accepted his father's one embrace stoically. Somehow, the warm feeling of their clothes and the flesh inside had stayed with him all that long day.

Ten hours for twenty kilometers, packed in with four other nervous, tight-lipped passengers with their bags and bundles. More than nine of those hours had passed as they waited at checkpoints, wondering if the rattling old taxi's gas would give out . . . fearing the scrutiny of the soldiers, who might delay them even further on some pretext or other.

One soldier, in dark glasses, had peered in at him and spoken in Arabic. "Getting out of the fighting, huh? Smart kid."

Mujahhid had wanted to flare up: *You think I want to? I'd throw something at* you, *if I could!* But of course he'd kept his mouth shut.

Now, at the home of his Aunt Rasheeda, Mujahhid sat with the family at the midday meal. Yesterday she had managed to find some chicken for his first dinner with them, but today they were back to yogurt and rice. Money was scarce, and good food scarcer.

He looked up from his empty plate and briefly studied the faces of the three women at the table. Aunt Rasheeda, tired and sallow, with short hair of a dark reddish color . . . she said little but kept the household going, while teaching at the village elementary school and working a second job in an office. Next to her sat the grandmother, whom they called Sitti, "Granny." Withered but bright-eyed, she wore a head scarf and her traditional long dress richly embroidered in bright colors, the dress she had made many years ago according to the old Palestinian custom. "She'll wear it till it falls apart," Mujahhid's cousin Hanan had told him. "She keeps part of Palestine alive that way."

And Hanan herself, a year older than Mujahhid, with thick black hair in a single braid and a sober face. Too many small blemishes to be really pretty, he thought, but okay. A good student, Hanan was aiming at medical school, and Mujahhid found her serious manner a little intimidating. He hoped she would properly appreciate his past role as a fighter for freedom, but feared she might see him as just a troublesome kid, something more for them to worry about. In general, he resolved to keep out of her way.

The meal was over. Having spent the morning doing odd jobs for his aunt, Mujahhid wanted to go out and see if there was anything interesting in this quiet little place, which he had seen previously only on brief family visits. Sitti, however, in a talkative mood, kept them at the table.

She made a sour face as she reached for the small dish of olives. "Old, last year's crop," she said, chewing with her few remaining teeth. "From our neighbor's trees . . . good enough, but never as good as our own."

Mujahhid allowed his face to show a flicker of surprise. He hadn't seen any olive trees on his aunt's property. The house was a small one built of plaster-covered cinder blocks, with barely enough yard for a patch of parsley and a clothesline.

"Not here," said Sitti, noticing. "I mean in the village. The old village, the one we left in '48. Every year at this time we used to go back—not supposed to, of course, but they didn't watch the back roads too closely then, not like they do now. We'd all squeeze in the car . . . my husband drove. He wouldn't pick the olives, though. Said it made him feel like he was stealing from his own land. He'd sit in the car and cry—I could tell—while the rest of us did the work. God bless him, stubborn old man."

"But," Mujahhid asked, puzzled, "how could you pick olives in the village you left so long ago?"

"Oh, there're lots of villages they never built on. Not yet, anyway. Drove the people out, tore down the houses, but left the trees and gardens. So we could still get the olives and the thyme and even some grapes, for a while." She sighed. "Oh, those olives were tasty, olives from heaven. God wanted us still to have them. God be praised, He still gives us the beauty of the world. He still gives us good, even in our loss. God is merciful."

God gives us olives, thought Mujahhid, *but took my brother and my best friend.* He shifted restlessly in his chair, wanting to say something but not knowing what. Then Aunt Rasheeda touched his arm.

"We have to talk more about olives, Mujahhid," she said. "Our neighbor still has a grove, thanks to God, and we must help him with the harvest. All of us. You'll be a big help, you're young and full of energy."

What was this? Mujahhid stared at his aunt. "But—but I don't know anything about picking olives. I've never done it before. I'd— how can I do that work?"

"You'll learn quickly enough, it's not hard. We need you, Mujahhid. They're ripe now."

Mujahhid pushed away from the table, stood, and with a muttered phrase of necessary politeness, left the room. It wasn't just the idea of physical work that riled him—although he had little experience other than helping in his father's shop. It was the thought of picking olives, something so ordinary, so dull, when he should be back in the city, carrying on the struggle in the name of his brother and friend. The shame of it tore at his insides. What would his friends say, who were bravely facing danger every day?

He went out to stand by the front gate of the house, feeling like a prisoner. In the peaceful quiet he scowled at his surroundings, the soft yellow of the stone houses warm in the afternoon sun. The village was called Beit al-Makhfiya, the "hidden place." Mujahhid didn't know why it was called that, but it was "nowhere" in his eyes, just a few narrow streets of small houses and, a short distance off, the olive grove.

Then, beyond the grove, he noticed something he had not seen before. On a nearby hilltop, overlooking the village homes, stood a tight cluster of new, boxlike buildings—a community of Jewish settlers. It looked as though it had been planted there by mistake, like a military fort in a garden. Anger started to smoke inside Mujahhid.

He heard someone approaching but didn't turn. In a moment Hanan spoke, in quiet tones.

"I couldn't say anything earlier, Mujahhid, it would just upset my mother. But, well, I want to say how sorry I am about your brother. He was so good, such a fine person."

Mujahhid gave her a fleeting glance. Maybe she'd been fond of his brother. . . . His heart felt contracted with his own grief, and now—it surprised him how quickly—with hers.

Hanan let out a sigh. "And sorry about your friend, of course."

Mujahhid's thoughts, forced back to the holes that had appeared so abruptly in his life, became confused and turbulent. He knew it was wrong to question, but he couldn't help wondering why God had let those terrible things happen. His family had always tried to be good Muslims, to love God and live as He wanted them to. But sometimes God made decisions that were very hard to understand.

They stood quietly for a minute or two. Then Hanan spoke again, in a different tone. "I know how you feel," she said. "I mean, about that, and about the olive picking. It really isn't hard, you know, and it'll take only a few days. The neighbor's old, he doesn't have enough help in his own family. We have to do it, Mujahhid."

"Why?" He turned on her. "To get your year's supply?" It was a rude reply, coming from his pain. But he didn't miss the tightening of Hanan's expression.

"He's generous, he lets us keep a lot," she answered coolly. "But that's not the only reason. Mama owes him money. Every year she has to borrow from him, and he lets her pay it back by helping with the olive harvest. She wouldn't want you to know that, of course, but I guess you need to. We've always had to do it alone and it's hard for us, especially Sitti. We really need your help, Mujahhid."

Stung, he remained silent. After a moment Hanan went on. "Olive trees mean so much to the villagers. Not just for food . . . but they're almost like children, something sacred. We feel that God gives them to sustain us, just as Sitti said."

Mujahhid thought, *sure, I know about olive trees. We have them in Bethlehem, too. But—*

"It's the only grove left around here. So many people in this area have lost their homes and their groves and orchards. Everything smashed and uprooted, to make roads for the Israelis, or because the army says people could hide among the trees. Just to suit . . . them." She finished with a glance and a shrug in the direction of the settlement.

"All right!" Mujahhid snapped suddenly. "I never said I wouldn't, did I? I'll pick a ton of olives, if that's what you want. It's just that—that I should be doing something else."

"What should you be doing?"

"The jihad! The holy struggle to win back our land!"

Hanan drew in her breath. It sounded almost like a sniff, and Mujahhid felt a prick of anger. "The fighting at the army checkpoint in Bethlehem," she said quietly. "I respect that, Mujahhid. But there's more than one kind of jihad."

"That's the only kind I want to fight!"

Then, again Mujahhid saw his friend Nawar lying motionless, heard the roar of tanks and helicopters and shells, the earsplitting racket of rifle fire. He felt cold with fear—and hot with the shame of his cowardice. God must find him disgusting.

Each morning, Mujahhid and Hanan walked several kilometers to a high school in a neighboring village. Afternoons they spent in the neighbor's olive grove. For four days Mujahhid worked alongside his cousin and one or both of the older women. He worked silently, half listening to their chatter and responding only with grunts when they spoke to him. Contrary to what Hanan had promised, it was hard work—beating the branches with a long stick so the women could pick up the olives that fell onto a cloth spread below. Mujahhid's arms and shoulders ached from the unfamiliar exercise. Furthermore, it felt like forced labor. When any of the villagers passed nearby, he kept his face turned away, not wanting anyone to think he was doing this willingly.

At times, however, he let himself weaken a bit. For a moment or two, lulled by the whisper of the silvery green leaves, he would run his hand lightly over the gnarled wood and think about how very old these trees were, the two or three hundred years they had seen on this quiet hillside, the many human lives they had nourished.

But then Mujahhid would catch himself. *Don't get silly,* he thought. *They're just old trees.*

On the fifth day he set out for the grove as soon as he got back from school. He was already tired after the long walk, but now anxious to finish the job. The crop was bountiful this year, and they had harvested only half the trees thus far.

Looking ahead, he saw Israeli soldiers in the road. Some of the neighbors had gathered, more than a dozen, mostly women.

Mujahhid paused, uncertain, wondering whether he dared confront the soldiers. In the streets of Bethlehem he had shouted himself hoarse at soldiers from a distance, yelling every curse, obscenity, and patriotic slogan he could think of. But he had rarely talked with a soldier, except for brief muttered answers when stopped at checkpoints. What would it be like to tell these men face to face: *Get out, leave us alone!*

He took a few steps, hesitated, then quickened his resolve and walked up to the nearest soldier. "What—what's going on?" he asked, embarrassed by the crack in his voice.

The soldier turned to Mujahhid. He looked young, less than twenty, with pink splotches on his cheeks and a small chin. His eyes were not hidden behind dark glasses, and Mujahhid was glad of that.

"These trees must be destroyed," the soldier said in heavily accented Arabic. "The bulldozers are coming any minute. These people must get out of the way."

For a moment Mujahhid could not believe what he had heard. Then he began to sputter, his determination to keep cool completely undone. "These—these olive trees—what d'you mean? Why?" The villagers backed him up with a raucous uproar.

The soldier winced and raised his voice. "I'm trying to explain—if you'd only be quiet! Listen, everyone, this orchard is in the way. A new road will go through here, a road to the settlement up there. The settlement needs a good road to Jerusalem. The olive trees are in the way. They must go." He spoke slowly, as though he were repeating simple information for children, but with a trace of uncertainty.

Mujahhid glanced at the trees nearby—and suddenly he felt that he was seeing them in a new way. Their oddly bent shapes, like old people, their delicate leaves dancing like soft young children, the ripe olives still glistening on the branches, like strong, confident youths. They seemed to be speaking to him, and at last he could hear. Sitti's words came back to him. . . . *God still gives us the beauty of the world, even in our loss.* At the time, he'd thought it was just old-woman talk. Now he understood. The olive grove was something fine that God in His goodness had made for people.

In a way, it was just as sacred as a mosque. The trees must be defended.

"You can't do that!" Mujahhid shouted in a burst of passion. "You can't cut down those trees! They don't belong to you—they're our neighbor's, and they're all he's got." Vaguely he became aware that the chorus of villagers' angry voices was subsiding, and in the quiet his voice rose. "You can't cut these trees! Go away—all of you, go away! This is *our village*!"

"Look, kid!" said the soldier, seeming more uneasy with every word. "It's not my idea. I don't decide to cut down trees—I don't like to cut down trees. I'm just following orders."

"They're bad orders. Go tell the army they're bad orders and you won't do them. We won't let you—we'll fight you!"

Mujahhid saw something like a veil of fear in the soldier's eyes, but the young man quickly mastered it. He was sweating, his hands nervously fidgeting as he held his rifle. Other soldiers, a half dozen or so, now joined him. He seemed to be the main spokesman, probably knowing Arabic better than the others.

"Kid, listen," stammered the soldier, his face taking on a look of earnestness. "It—it won't do you any good. This has to be done. Come on, be reasonable, go on home and let us get on with it—"

One of the other soldiers broke in. In a glance, Mujahhid saw that the man had a superior rank, probably the sergeant in charge of the detail. He barked at the younger man in Hebrew, then turned and gave Mujahhid a swift cuff on the side of the head.

"Get out, Arab filth."

Hurt, furious, Mujahhid staggered and nearly fell. But as he turned away, he caught sight of a flash of color among the more distant olive trees. What could that be? Sitti? . . . Yes, Sitti, in her embroidered dress! And Hanan with her. Somehow they must have gotten into the olive grove unnoticed from a terrace higher up the hillside. In that instant, Mujahhid knew that the battle was not yet over.

He retreated from the soldiers, rubbing his temple where the sergeant had hit him. Head low, he started to shuffle away toward the nearest houses. A moan rose from the crowd, a sigh of disappointment before the women started their haranguing again.

As soon as Mujahhid felt safely out of the soldiers' view, he dashed around the corner of a house and raced back to the upper terrace of the olive grove. Reaching it, he climbed over a stone wall, as his cousin and grandmother must have done, and soon joined them.

They greeted him with nods and promptly resumed their work. Mujahhid fell into their rhythm, the pace at which they'd always worked . . . not so fast as to tire early, not so slow as to needlessly prolong the job. He pulled down and held the branches so Hanan could gather the olives into her bamboo basket. Steadily, calmly, they went on with the harvest.

Suddenly an angry shout went up from the soldiers. Then came a collective cheer from the villagers. Mujahhid tried to ignore both. But from the corner of his eye he could see someone hurrying toward them, dodging around the trees. A moment later the young soldier reached Mujahhid and took him by the arm.

"Kid, get your sister and granny out of here!" blurted the soldier. "They can get hurt—I don't want them to get hurt! Or *you*— and you will, if you—"

Hanan broke in. "The olives have to be harvested," she said matter-of-factly, as though speaking to a grocer. "There's no sense letting them go to waste."

Shooting a look of admiration at her, Mujahhid took the cue. "This is our job. We have to get on with it."

"*Yallah,* young man," said Sitti to the soldier, "make yourself useful or make yourself scarce. We've got work to do." She bent over to pick up a few olives that had fallen to the dry soil.

The Israeli turned back to Mujahhid. "Look, you think I like this? Tearing down trees, knocking people around? Is this right, destroying the world God gave us—"

At an angry shout, he jumped and glanced around nervously. His sergeant and a few other soldiers were hurrying toward them. The young soldier seized Mujahhid by the shoulders and pleaded once more.

"You've got to get out of here! Please, before you get hurt! *Please!*"

But Mujahhid stood motionless, startled and held by the soldier's words: "*. . . destroying the world God gave us. . . .*"

The men reached them. Hesitating in confusion for a moment, the soldier then turned from Mujahhid, rushed over and stood by the two women, his arms outstretched protectively. Two of the other soldiers shoved him away. They seized Sitti and Hanan, knocked the baskets from their hands, and propelled them swiftly along the stony terraces toward the road.

With a shout of protest Mujahhid started toward his cousin and grandmother, only to find himself again grabbed by the young soldier. This time, however, the soldier seemed to be trying to keep Mujahhid away from the other men. It did no good. Mujahhid felt himself yanked from the soldier's grasp. Holding him by his shirt front, the sergeant slapped him hard several times, on both sides of the head, then threw him face down with full force.

Mujahhid lay on the stony ground, his head ringing from the blows. But above him he heard a verbal battle begin to break out. The younger soldier, impassioned, yelled in Hebrew at his sergeant.

The sergeant, equally enraged, shouted back. Although he could not understand the furious words, Mujahhid grasped the meaning and heard the young soldier ordered away.

As Mujahhid tried to pull himself up, someone yanked him to his feet. For a second, before steel-like hands started to drag him through the grove, he caught a last glimpse of the young soldier . . . cheeks flaming, face twisted with anger and shame. Their eyes met, and Mujahhid understood something more. Maybe he and that soldier were not so very far apart.

At the washbasin by the kitchen, Hanan helped clean the dirt from Mujahhid's face, gently sponging the dark bruises. No way to conceal them from Aunt Rasheeda, of course. She would learn all about it anyway, as soon as she got home from work. Even now they could hear the growl of bulldozers at the other end of the village, and the death groans of the old trees.

Mujahhid turned from Hanan's hands and studied his face in the cracked mirror over the sink. Battle scars . . . he was proud of them. And thankful not to have a bullet in his throat, like Nawar. He didn't think he really wanted to be a martyr. It was better to live, to go on with the struggle.

And then, as Hanan pulled his face around to apply ointment to the abrasions, he seemed to hear again her earlier words. *There's more than one kind of jihad, you know. Yes,* Mujahhid thought, *I guess I do know now. Doing whatever you have to do—like picking olives—when you have to do it. Or standing up for what you think is right. Doing it no matter what. Maybe that's the kind of jihad God really wants from us. From* all *of us.*

5

In Line

A STORY FROM EGYPT

Halfway home from school, on a lovely clear day in December, I did something really daring. I decided to change my route. Not much, of course, because my mother knew exactly how long it took me to get home and she would be waiting. I just thought it would be nice to walk along the canal a bit and pretend it was the Nile. That's how it happened I ran into Fayza.

I'd noticed her in class. You could hardly not notice her, even in a classroom as packed with people as ours. She always raised her hand to answer the teacher's questions—she even asked good questions of her own! What's more, she was a lot smarter than most of the boys and wasn't afraid to let them know it. So I'd begun to think I'd like to get to know her. But how? Most people still acted as if I were from Mars, or someplace even farther away, and they couldn't figure me out. I was afraid Fayza might feel that way, too.

Well, I would try, at least.

Fayza was standing at the edge of the canal, holding a big bunch of flowers—roses so bedraggled they looked as though the flower seller had given them to her for free. But what made me curious was the way she was staring down at the canal. I stopped near her to see what she was looking at. It was a donkey, dead, lying there in the water.

"Ugh! How awful!" I said. "Why do they allow that?" I couldn't help it, bursting out like that even before saying hello. Such an ugly sight, flies and everything!

"Ugh is right, Rania," Fayza said, barely glancing at me. "It's stupid, and bad for health. And besides, it's sad. Poor donkey, he wasn't even very old."

It didn't surprise me that she knew my name—the teacher had called on me often enough. But what Fayza said about the dead donkey being sad did surprise me. Dead animals were common in the countryside, and nobody seemed to care much, so far as I could tell. Why should she feel sad?

"Anyway," I said, "it would have had a hard life."

Fayza sighed. "Of course. But I still think it's too bad for animals to die so miserably. I wish all creatures could have happy lives, people and animals both. I think that's what God wants."

I looked at her, wondering. She was quite pretty, with gray eyes and her hair in braids. Then I had an idea—although it was a little bold of me since we didn't even know each other.

"Maybe you should become a veterinarian," I said.

For the first time she looked up at me and smiled. "Yes! Yes, that's exactly what I want to do. Go to veterinary college and then work in a village or town somewhere around here. Maybe I can make life a little better, someday."

Imagine already knowing what you want to do in life! And something that would be very useful, like helping farmers keep their animals healthy. The kids I knew in Cairo—all they thought about was music and the cinema and having a big birthday party at a hotel.

Fayza sighed again. "I have to get home now." But as she started to leave the canal, she paused and turned back. She broke off a couple of droopy rosebuds and tossed them down onto the donkey.

What a thing to do—scatter flowers on a dead animal! But a moment later, hardly knowing I was doing it, I broke off one of her roses. "Let me, too."

Again Fayza grinned at me, and then we both tried to look very solemn and sad. We tossed flowers with great ceremony until that big bunch was all gone, and the donkey was covered with pink and yellow rosebuds.

"For sure, that donkey needs them more than my family does," said Fayza.

"At least we've given him a proper funeral." I was so surprised at myself for what I'd done that I had to smile—and we both began to laugh. Then we said good-bye and I went on my way. I kept thinking, what would my mother do if she knew I'd thrown rosebuds onto a dead donkey? Probably sterilize my hands!

So that was how Fayza and I became friends. A funeral made me start to feel alive again. Until that day, I'd felt as though I were stuck in the mud that fills the village streets after a hard rain.

Actually, nobody in our family had been happy about my father's getting assigned to a small village in the flat, nothing-happening Delta. But that's what happens when you work for the government. This village needed a social services coordinator, so the government sent him. It was a huge change from our life in Cairo, and my mother could hardly bear it. No job for her, no friends, nothing she liked to do. Sometimes she said to me, with a deep sigh, "Rania, I am a fish far from the Nile." I couldn't blame her.

My brother Ameen soon became buddies with the school principal's son—changes aren't too tough when you're only nine.

But it wasn't so easy for me at thirteen. I think the village girls and boys took my shyness for snobbishness and thought I was looking down at them. That's why, after four months of being by myself, I was so glad to get to know Fayza.

From then on, we spent time together every day at school, talking about all sorts of things—classwork, our families, and all the things we wished we could do someday. Then one day Fayza asked if I could come to her house for lunch. I was so happy! But I knew it would take some doing to get my mother to agree.

We were in the kitchen, where my mother was making *kousa mahshi,* carefully hollowing out dozens of little squashes and stuffing them with rice and meat. Leaning against the door frame, I watched her work and wished I could help, because she looked tired. But I knew if I offered to help, she'd just tell me to run along and do my homework. I didn't want to take that chance, so I hung around, trying to work up the courage to ask my big question. She beat me to it.

"Rania, who is this girl you've been talking about? I want to know more about her." She spoke pleasantly, but I knew it wasn't just casual interest.

I didn't answer right away, trying to recall what I might have said about Fayza. Not much, I was sure; just that I'd met someone I could talk with.

"I asked you a question," my mother said, wiping her sticky hands on her apron and turning to look at me. "Tell me about this girl Fayza Hamada."

"She's . . . I told you, Mummy, she's in my class," I said. "And she's smart. She always knows the right answer. More than any of the boys—that should please you. And she's nice. I like her."

"Well, fine. But what do you know about her family? If her father were the mayor or the doctor or agronomist, we would surely know the family. No family we know has a daughter named Fayza."

It was just as I'd feared. If my mother had her way, I'd be friends only with girls from families like ours. But I was a teenager now, so why couldn't I choose my own friends?

Trying to cover up my feelings, I gave a little shrug. "Fayza's father is a farmer, Mummy, like most everybody else. He has chickens and a donkey and a cow. He raises cotton. That's what people do around here, you know." A warning look in my mother's eye made me stop short. She didn't appreciate smart talk.

"Oh," she said and turned back to the squashes. "Well, that's what I was expecting, of course. So Fayza is a good student . . . that's nice. I hope they're not planning to marry her off at fourteen."

Really! As if all the peasants in Egypt were still living in the time of the pharaohs! "No, Mummy, I don't think so," I said, managing to keep calm. "They're proud that she does so well in school. She tells me so."

"Very good. Well," my mother went on, "what can you find to talk about with a girl like Fayza? Has she ever been outside the village?"

I nearly snorted with exasperation. "We talk about lots of things. Mostly school, of course. And we read books together."

That seemed to satisfy my mother for the moment. She went on working at the stone counter. I noticed she was shifting her weight a lot because of her aching legs. Something to do with "very close veins," as she said every evening when she sat down to relax in front of the television. In that tiny kitchen, though, there was no place where she could sit and work, and I always felt sorry that it was so hard for her.

Watching my mother, I recalled the one time when Fayza and I stopped—just for a minute—at the Hamadas' house on the way home from school. Her mother was shelling peas, squatting on the hard-packed dirt outside their mud-brick house. Now I got a silly idea: it might be better for my mother's veins if she squatted on the floor to work! But I kept my mouth shut. Mummy wouldn't think that was funny at all.

"Now, dear," she said, as I knew she soon would, "you run along and get started on your homework. I'm sure you have plenty to do."

I let out a sigh, disappointed that I hadn't been able to ask my big question. And I was mad at myself for not having more courage.

"Oh, now don't sigh, it can't be as bad as all that," my mother said. "As soon as I get dinner prepared, I'll come and help you with your English. At least that's one thing I can do with my honors degree in English literature, you lucky girl," she added with a smile. "You must be well ahead of all the other students. By the way, what about Fayza? How does she do in English?"

I perked up—maybe this was my chance. "Oh, she's good! And sometimes we help each other." Then I went on in a rush, before I lost my nerve. "Mummy, Fayza has asked me to come to her house sometime for lunch. In fact, she said maybe next Friday. Would that be all right?" I watched my mother's face closely, to see how she would react to this startling idea.

Her lips pursed a bit. "Oh . . . I'm not sure about that, dear."

Well, she hadn't actually said no, so I pumped up my courage and tried again. "Do you and Daddy have anything else planned for Friday? If you don't, then, please, could I? I'd really like to—and her family wants me to come. Please, Mummy, *please*?"

She frowned, and I could imagine her weighing out the good things and the bad things. Would she have to meet Fayza's family—and would she have to extend a return invitation? What would people think about the daughter of the senior social services officer, a government official from Cairo, being entertained in a peasant home? Really, was this friendship something to be encouraged?

At last my mother's face eased into a little smile. "Oh, very well, Rania, you may. But . . . well, you know. I'll expect you to use good judgment at all times. Wash your hands very carefully before you eat anything, of course, and peel everything."

Ya salaam! I could hardly believe it! "Of course, Mummy, of course!" I was so happy that I hugged her and ran out of the kitchen—and did a super job on my homework.

All week I looked forward to Friday. Fayza would come to meet my mother around noon, and then we'd go to her house. I waited for her at the door to the building so the *bawwab* wouldn't shoo her away—he took his door-guarding duties too seriously, the silly man. I'd been hoping she'd wear the school uniform of gray slacks and sweater, but she was in her village clothes, a long dress of colorful printed cotton, faded and a little outgrown, but freshly laundered.

When we got up to the flat, I saw that Mummy had put on eye makeup and the *hijab,* as she did whenever she went out. It was a fancy headcovering of white fabric with fringe, which covered all her hair—the Islamic thing, not like the little scarves that the village women wore.

Mummy greeted Fayza politely and smiled graciously, but I wanted to get out of there quickly before she started to ask Fayza questions. So I acted jumpy and impatient, and we said good-bye, hustled down the stairs, and scooted out into the street.

For a few minutes we didn't talk, even though I was full of excitement. Fayza seemed nervous and unsure. Then she said, "Your mother is very beautiful. Her headcovering is elegant."

"Thank you." I tried not to show what I was thinking. Not being a very religious person, Mummy hardly ever wore the *hijab* at home. So why now? It was almost as though she wanted to say to

Fayza, "Please take note, I'm a sophisticated lady from the city. I'm different from the other women around here."

There was another short, awkward pause before Fayza spoke again. "Rania," she said, "I have to do some work at home first. . . . I'm sorry. But then we can be free to do what we want. It's not much work, just gathering the eggs and bringing fodder for the cow." She looked a little worried, as if she wasn't sure how I would take that news.

It sounded like fun to me! "Okay, I'll help you," I said.

"You?" Fayza looked at me and laughed. "That'll be a sight, you lugging fodder in those nice clothes. No, you can wait in the shade. *Umma* will give you a cool drink."

"No, I really want to! I've never collected eggs before, but I'm sure I have a secret talent for finding them. You'll see."

That made Fayza giggle, and we began to feel better.

When we reached her house, Mrs. Hamada was waiting with a big smile that showed one gold tooth. She was wearing a wrinkled little black kerchief over her hair and a loose, faded flowered dress down to her ankles, like most of the village women. Fayza called her mother *Umma* and told me to say Um-Sayid, "mother of Sayid." She'd spoken to me a few times about her older brother Sayid, what a show-off and know-it-all he was, and I wondered whether I'd have to meet the obnoxious boy himself.

Soon we got to work looking for eggs in every corner of the yard. We made a treasure hunt of it, shouting over every egg we found, while Um-Sayid stood in the low doorway of the house, laughing until her large body shook all over.

Next, Fayza took me out to the fields of berseem. I'd never been close to a field of berseem before. It's such a pretty plant, with leaves like bright green clover. I thought it must make the cows feel very happy.

"Now Rania," Fayza said firmly, "you just watch while I fix lunch for the cow. Really, you must. Hunting for eggs is one thing, gathering berseem is another."

"No, please! I want to do it, too. Show me how," I said.

I really wanted to get into that field and be surrounded by all that lush green stuff. Fayza frowned at me, not just squinting in the bright sun but as if she didn't know what to make of me. And I admit it was silly, but that was the way I felt.

"This is messy, Rania," she said. "You'll get your clothes dirty—look, there's already some mud on your jeans."

"Then it won't matter if I get a little dirtier." After all, when would I have a chance like this again?

Shaking her head, Fayza said with a giggle, "I think you're crazy. Well, come on."

We got to work cutting the plants and carrying armloads through the dusty fields, trying to stay out of muddy patches where the rows had been recently irrigated. It was harder work than I'd thought, but it was still fun.

Then we lugged all that stuff back to the cow, who was kept in a little pen next to the house. Suddenly the cow let out a huge bellow, and I jumped halfway out of my shoes! I wasn't used to animals—in Cairo I'd seen only stray cats and dogs, and horses pulling carts. That cow looked awfully big and unpredictable. Fayza, though, was perfectly at ease, stroking and talking to the animal, as though it were a friend. It reminded me of the day we met by the canal and how she'd felt sad about the dead donkey.

I kept my distance as the cow munched the berseem, and then we went to the house. By then I was more than a little dirty. Fayza got a basin of water and tried to scrub the mud off my new pink top, but she only made it worse.

"No problem," I said—those English words are so useful for

Egyptians!—and we both laughed. But I knew very well that when I got home, my dirty clothes definitely *would* be a problem.

Finally lunchtime came for the whole family. I was really hungry—but as I stepped inside the main room of the house, I felt baffled. Where was the dining table? A narrow bench with a thin cushion ran along three walls, but there was no table. Then I realized that I should sit down on the ground—there were mats spread out—in a circle with everyone else. We each had a plate, and in the middle of the circle sat a large pot of stewed chicken with lots of onions and garlic, and a heaping platter of stuffed cabbage leaves. Everyone dug in and ate without ceremony. I couldn't help thinking how different it all was from home, where my mother set the table with style and care, made sure everything was clean, and kept reminding Ameen and me of our manners.

Fayza's younger brother and sister sat near their mother. Directly across from me, beside his father, sat the notorious First Son, Sayid. To be perfectly truthful, I could hardly keep myself from staring at him. He was only fourteen, but he looked already almost like a man, with broad shoulders and a square jaw. And he didn't act like a show-off at all. In fact, he didn't say a word. And it seemed he kept staring at me. Every time I caught him, he'd immediately drop his gaze. Finally he smiled.

Um-Sayid noticed—not much got past her!—and laughed. "We don't see many city people here, Rania," she said, "and the children have never met a city girl their own age. They're too curious, I'm afraid. Please excuse them."

"It's all right," I murmured, feeling my face get hot. After all, I was the one being curious, but Um-Sayid was so tactful. And when she talked about our treasure hunt, and Fayza told about my being scared of the cow, they all laughed—but never made me feel like a dumb city person. After we ate the chicken, they offered me a bowl of figs, which were very expensive because it was late in the season. I knew they'd bought them just for me. Then they gave me the very best of the tangerines. I felt so full I didn't think I could get up off the floor.

Later, as Fayza and I walked back to my house, I thought, *Oh, I hope God will give me more days like this one! It had been just perfect, cow and all.*

I was still feeling so good when I got home, I gave my mother a big hug. "*Umma, Umma, Umma!* I had such a good time!"

"Wonderful, darling, I'm glad you had fun," she said. Then she pushed me away a little and looked at me curiously. "But tell me, why am I suddenly *Umma*?"

"That's what Fayza calls her mother," I said. "That's what all the girls call their mothers here."

My mother gave a short laugh. "Well, dearie, all the girls in the *village*. In this house, you just go on calling me Mummy, as you always have. That's what I learned when I was a child, at my English school. That's what *we* say. And now, let's have a look at you." She stepped back, holding me at arm's length. "Oh my, your clothes are a sight! However did you get so dirty?"

"Helping Fayza," I answered, trying my best to keep up the happy mood that I'd come home with. "We gathered eggs, and then we cut berseem for the cow, and it was fun—but just a little muddy in places, and—"

"You went into the fields? You had to do that work?"

"Had to—? No, Mummy, I *wanted* to! Fayza told me I'd better not, she was worried about my clothes getting dirty, but I wanted to. I told you, it was fun!"

"Really, dear?" she said in that way that means *not* really. "It seems very strange to me that you'd want to spend your time working in the fields—or that they'd allow you to. This is not at all what

I expected." She shook her head, frowning, and focused on my clothes again. "That big stain is not going to be easy to get out. And that's the nice little top that your Aunt Sadiyya sent you from Cairo. What a pity. *Really,* dear."

That made me feel just wonderful. And Mummy could see that she'd made me unhappy, so she tried to be nicer and smiled again. "Well, what was lunch like? What did Madame Hamada serve?"

It did cheer me up a little, remembering how everyone had made me feel so welcome . . . and how Sayid and I had kept looking at each other. "Oh, it was good!" I said. "We all sat around on the floor, and we all took what we wanted from a big pot, and . . . it was very good."

How dumb can you get? Why couldn't I have just said "chicken stew and stuffed cabbage leaves" and let it go at that? From the look on my mother's face, clearly it didn't sound "very good" to her.

Sure enough, the next day as we were setting the dinner table together, she told me that I should have friends come to *my* house from now on. "This way, you see, dear," she said, "we can be sure of cleanliness. There are still so many diseases that people can get in the village, we just can't be too careful."

I dropped a fork on the table and stared at her. "But—but nobody was sick at—"

"In fact, *habeebti,* dearie," she went on, straightening the fork, "you must soon start preparing for your exams, you know. The New Year holiday is coming up, and we're invited to Cairo to visit Uncle Mourad and Aunt Sadiyya. Then it'll be exam time and you must get top grades, you know, Rania. We've spent so much money for the extra tutoring that your father and I have a right to expect a lot from you."

Oh, I knew that, all right. It was Topic Number One in our family. "I *am* getting good marks," I said. "Mummy, listen—"

"It's your whole future, dear. You're not too young to be think-ing of the General Secondary Exam, even though it's still a few years away. Everything depends on that—whether you go on to the university at a high level, or have to settle for second-rate. None of us want that, do we, dear?" She looked up at me, and I could see that she wasn't just laying down the law. She was almost begging me not to disappoint her.

"I know, I know!" I said. "But—"

The moment passed, and Mummy became the lady in charge again. "Besides, any extra time you have, you should try to help your brother. These years are all for preparation, dear, not for frit-tering away. Competition is terribly tough in this world, and later on you'll be thankful you didn't let yourself get distracted from your work."

I couldn't think of anything to say. I felt like a stuffed animal with all the cotton falling out. So now, I thought, will my life be like it was before I met Fayza and started to be happy here? Nothing but school and tutoring and studying?

"Just think how lucky you are," my mother went on. "The fu-ture of a girl like Fayza—even though she might be very smart—is so limited. But you can prepare for anything you want, be a doctor or architect or university professor, anything."

For a moment I saw a chance to speak my mind. "I don't think Fayza's future will be so bad. She's ambitious and—"

But my mother only nodded. "You'll see the truth of what I'm saying."

And that was that. I finished setting the table and hurried to my room to be miserable.

In the winter weeks that followed, Fayza and I were as friendly as ever at school. Three times I asked her to come to my house after school or on Friday, but Fayza always had some reason why she couldn't: extra work at home or going to visit relatives. Finally I gave up, because I was afraid that Fayza simply didn't want to come to my home. She knew she wouldn't really be welcome in my mother's house.

On the days when rain fell from heavy gray skies and turned the whole world into mud, I sat at my study table and brooded. I wished I could be in Fayza's little house, no matter how chilly it might be. I could imagine the men making jokes and Um-Sayid snapping back funny remarks that made everybody laugh and forget the cold, and sometimes I could almost hear Fayza's giggle. But I could only pretend. Everything that would make me happy seemed to be ruled out.

Then one sunny day in late January, something nice came my way. My father had been in Cairo, and when he returned, he had a package for me.

Skates! In-line skates! I shrieked, I was so excited. "Oh, Daddy, thank you! Blue and silver—just like the ones we saw in that store in Cairo, Mummy, remember?"

"Actually," she said, "they're a gift from your aunt Sadiyya."

"Oh, how nice of her!"

"Yes, your aunt Sadiyya is certainly very kind. She's always thinking of you . . . and of course she has the means to make nice little gifts, too." Then my mother gave a wry smile. "Although where she thinks you're going to use these skates in a village, I can't imagine. The streets are all either dust or mud."

For a moment I felt my own smile fading, but quickly I got an idea. "I know where—the place where Daddy works! The government compound has a concrete yard, and I can skate there."

My parents looked at each other and agreed. "Why, yes," Mummy said, "perhaps you could. We'll go there sometime soon, when the offices are closed."

That sounded fine to me. But a little later, as I was examining the skates and thinking how wonderful it would be to whiz around with all that silver on my feet, I thought of Fayza. She would love to try those skates! What good was a wonderful new gift if you couldn't share it with a friend? It would be no fun at all, skating around all by myself, with only my mother for company.

So I made up my mind. I wouldn't wait for that "sometime soon"—I'd do it my own way. I'd been waiting long enough for a break from all my hard studying, waiting long enough for some *fun*. It seemed so right and so fair that I put aside any doubts.

After lunch on Friday afternoon, as soon as my parents were lying down for a nap, I slipped out of the apartment with the new skates tucked under my arm in a plastic bag. I hadn't breathed a word about what I was planning to do—not even to Ameen, though I knew he would have wanted to try the skates, too. Well, he'd have a chance later.

I hurried through the village streets, half afraid that I might have forgotten the way to Fayza's house. It had been so long since that wonderful day when I was there for lunch. I found it without any trouble, though, and Fayza was at home.

"Rania!" Fayza shouted, hugging me hard. Then, when she saw the skates, she shrieked even more. "They're beautiful! Oh, you lucky girl! Do you really know how to skate?"

"Sure, it's easy," I said. "I saw girls skating in Cairo loads of times. Come on, we'll try them together."

"Me, too? I can try them?" Fayza squealed, clapped her hands like a little kid, and ran inside to ask her mother.

When Um-Sayid came out of the house, her eyes grew big at the sight of my skates. "But you can't skate here," she said, looking around the dirt yard. "Where are you going to use them?"

"The government compound," I said. "It's concrete there."

107

"Your mama knows?"

"Yes, she knows." Which was true in a way . . . she knew the government compound was the only place we could skate.

Since I seemed to know my way around the government buildings so well, Um-Sayid said we could go, and we set off through the quiet streets. There wasn't anyone at the compound when we got there. Everyone had the day off, of course, and was probably home napping, like my parents. The concrete courtyard looked a bit bumpy, but it was certainly better than a muddy street.

I put on the skates first. I stood up—and they shot right out from under me! I landed hard on my seat. Again I tried, and again I fell. It wasn't easy at all! I scrambled to get upright again, wobbled and teetered, waving my arms. "I'm like a cow on a tightrope!" I shrieked, and went down again.

Fayza hooted with laughter. So I turned the skates over to her, and then it was my turn to laugh. But no matter how many times we fell and bruised our knees and elbows, at least we were doing it together—and that made it fun. I refused to even think about what I'd say to my mother later.

Before long, we heard excited shouts, and two young kids came running into the compound—Fayza's little sister and brother. "*Umma* told us you were here!" they yelled, jumping up and down. "Show us how you skate!"

What a nuisance! Why did those kids have to come? They'd just make a lot of racket and get in the way.

But then I saw who was with them. Sayid, looking tall and handsome in a clean galabiya. My heart dropped. Oh, I *can't* skate in front of *him*! I thought in dismay. I guess it's all over now.

I just stood there feeling mad and confused, while the little kids started bickering about the skates. But Sayid, with a smile, elbowed them aside. "My turn next," he said, making a deep bow to me. "With your permission, my lady. Would you permit me?"

"Y-you can try," I stammered, starting to laugh in spite of myself. "If you can get them on."

"Yes, just try, Sayid," said Fayza with a toss of her head. "You can't get even your big toe into these skates. And anyway, you'd make a bigger fool of yourself than we are."

Sitting on a concrete bench, Sayid pretended to struggle with a skate, then gave up and handed it to me. "Let me see you do it, Rania. You're sure to do better than my clumsy sister."

My face grew hot. It would be so embarrassing to fall or flop around awkwardly, waving my arms! But there was no way I could refuse.

"I'll try," I mumbled, putting on the skates again. "But I'm not really very good."

A miracle! I didn't fall down. Even with Sayid watching, suddenly I seemed to get the knack of it and keep my balance. I started to roll forward, and soon I could make a complete tour around the courtyard. Catching hold of one of the skinny trees that grew in a little island of soil in the concrete, I coasted in a semicircle. Fayza and Sayid began to sing a popular song, clapping loudly in time, and the children cheered—"*Yallah*, Rania! Go, Rania!"—until the whole government compound echoed.

Why, I could do it! Giddy with success, I skated with more speed and headed for Fayza and Sayid.

But when I'd almost reached them, a rough patch in the concrete caught my skate. I lost my balance, let out a shriek, and fell— right against Sayid! Down we both went. Sayid quickly jumped to his feet and gave me his hand to pull me up.

Suddenly, "*Rania! Rania Gamal!*"

I sat down hard again. The courtyard became deathly silent.

"So, my daughter, you did come here."

"Yes, Mummy . . . ," I said, turning toward her. "I—I just couldn't wait."

"And you didn't tell me. I can see why."

"Well, I . . . Mummy, I can do it!" With a spurt of hope—maybe I could distract her a bit—I babbled on. "I really can, Mummy. It's not easy, but I learned how—"

"That's beside the point, Rania. You were wrong to do this. Very, very wrong."

At that point she looked up—and focused on Sayid. He had already stepped away from me, but it did no good. I saw disapproval and anger in my mother's eyes. A young man—a *peasant*—behaving in such a casual way toward her daughter!

Fayza took the two kids by the hand and turned to her brother. "Come, Sayid," she said in a low voice. "We must go now."

He looked flushed with embarrassment. But as he started to leave, he paused for a moment. "Rania, are you all right? You are not hurt?"

"I'm all right," I answered, keeping my face down to hide the tears. The others left, and my mother and I walked home in silence.

At school the next day, I was afraid that Fayza might be upset and not want to talk to me. But she signaled me in class, and we got together at the first break. "Don't worry," I told her, somehow managing to keep a smile on my face. "My mother wasn't really angry. Everything's all right. But . . ." It wasn't, really. And I had to tell her what had been decided. "My parents say I absolutely have to study for exams now, nothing else. I must come home right after school every day."

Fayza sighed, and I knew she understood what that meant. "Yes, of course," she said quietly. "My mother keeps nagging me, too." From then on we had little time for each other.

On the day of the last midwinter exams, however, after we were all finished, Fayza and I left the school building together. Then I broke my news.

"I can't. . . ." Even though I'd rehearsed, it was hard to say. I had to swallow to ease my tight throat. "I won't be coming back to school, Fayza. I'm going to Cairo to live with my uncle Mourad and aunt Sadiyya. I have to leave tomorrow."

Fayza stopped short. When she spoke, her voice sounded carefully controlled. It was that very flatness of her voice that told me she felt the same way I did. "Well," she said, not looking at me, "you should go to a really good school, and now you can."

"Yes. A school for girls only. My parents think it's best." I sighed, scuffing my feet in the dirt. "But I wish things could be different."

"So do I." Fayza paused. Then she said, "Anyway, you are very smart, so you must go to the university and become a professor."

"And you, too, Fayza. You must learn to be a veterinarian. Think of all the poor donkeys waiting for you to take care of them." I tried to laugh a little but gave it up and turned to her seriously. "Fayza, will you write to me? I'll write to you."

"Of course! I will—" She stopped, distracted, because I had put down my backpack and was starting to pull out something bulky.

"I hope so," I said. "Because I want you to tell me—" I pushed the skates into Fayza's hands—"how you're doing on these!"

I didn't know how she'd take it. Maybe she would hate the skates, because of that awful scene in the government compound. But I could only hope she'd remember the fun that we'd had first.

Anyway, I wanted to do it, and before Fayza could say anything, I picked up my backpack and ran out of the school yard. At the gate I paused for only a quick wave.

In Cairo I would have been able to use those nice skates a lot. How would I explain to my mother and Aunt Saddiya what I had done? Well, I knew the answer: just tell the truth. I could already hear in my mind the shocked surprise, the disapproval, the disappointment. But it was a small price to pay, I felt, for my right to give my friend something nice . . . something that would help me be remembered.

As I hurried home through the muddy village streets, another thought came to me. I was stepping out of line, a little. And I liked it.

6

Scenes in a Roman Theater

A STORY FROM TUNISIA

With a sigh, Hedi plunked himself down on a stone seat in the Roman theater. As the last of the afternoon's tourists straggled off and disappeared among the ancient walls, he stared dully at the grand view of the ruins and the green hills of the Tunisian countryside beyond.

He hadn't done very well today. Only one hat sold. His mother would be disappointed, and he wouldn't blame her . . . having to make those hats every night after her day's labor in the fields, weaving straw till her fingers were sore. Tomorrow he'd try harder. Midwinter break from school gave him a few days to earn money, and he couldn't waste the chance.

It'd be so much better, Hedi often thought, if he could be a guide, more interesting and more money. Once in a while he did manage to latch on to a friendly couple and show them a few sights . . . the temple, the theater, the baths and marketplace—and best of all, the communal toilet where twelve people could sit at a time. That always got a laugh, and Hedi would get a few small coins. But that was all. A real guide had to be older and know a lot more.

So Hedi was stuck selling hats in the ruins of a once-glorious ancient town and wishing he could see something else of the world. His parents held out no hope of that, as year after year they struggled to make a living from two small wheat fields. But Hedi had a plan. In a couple of years he would quit school and go to work in one of the big seaside resorts, like his brother Tawfiq. He let his imagination drift in that direction now . . . an exciting life in a land of fancy hotels, rich people with big cars . . . and money.

His attention snapped back. Two boys, one carrying a couple of straw hats and the other a tray of small souvenir trinkets, were climbing toward him up the theater's worn steps. Tahar and Azouz, schoolmates of Hedi's, an inseparable pair. Approaching, they sneered at his stack of unsold hats.

"Some salesman you are," said Tahar, knocking it over with his foot.

Hedi rescued the hats and tried to give an indifferent shrug as the others sat down near him. They pulled candy bars from their pockets and began to eat ostentatiously without offering him a piece. Tahar and Azouz always did better than Hedi, in school and in the Roman ruins. They knew how to amuse the tourists—or make pests of themselves until their victims bought a hat or an ancient fake just to get rid of them.

Now Hedi noticed two more people entering the theater. Awkwardly laden with various items, they looked purposeful, not like tourists. The man set down a small stool and arranged a wooden sticklike contraption. He spoke to the woman and soon left with long-legged strides. The woman looked around as if selecting a view, then placed a white square on the easel, sat down, and started taking things from a large cloth bag. Watching from his stone seat higher up, Hedi understood. Artists liked to paint ruins.

"Here's your chance to sell a hat, Hedi," said Azouz in a mockingly sweet voice. "Or are you too shy?"

The words stung Hedi as though he'd been pushed into a cactus. Well, why not try? He'd show those pests. Followed closely by Azouz and Tahar, he hopped down the steps, climbed up on the stage, and approached the woman.

"*Chapeau, madame? Très bon, la qualité supérieur . . .*"

His words faltered as the woman pulled a floppy pink hat from her satchel and put it on. She was Tunisian, of middle age, dressed in jeans and a man's shirt with dabs of color on it. Glancing up at him, she answered in Arabic.

"No, boys, I don't need a hat. Run along now, please, I'm busy."

With effort, Hedi tried again. "Ah, madame, you need a better hat. Look, look at my hats, the very best. Don't buy anything cheap, madame. I assure you these are the best quality—my mother makes them, so I know. They'll keep the sun off, keep your skin nice. . . ." He blathered on, conscious of the other boys' smirks.

Azouz and Tahar now pushed Hedi aside and took over. They begged, laughed, bombarded the woman with questions. They pretended to stick their fingers in the paint on her palette and then decorate each other's faces. She smiled slightly at first but soon dropped any pretense of amusement.

"Boys, *yallah*! I have to work. Please!"

Hedi caught the nervous edge to her voice. Not content with goading *him* on, only to show him up as a fool, now Azouz and Tahar were getting under the woman's skin.

Again she protested, her voice rising, but it just inspired them to mimic. Finally, with a huff of exasperation, she took a roll of plastic film from her basket and started to spread it over the paint-laden palette. Hedi watched, feeling more and more angry at the two boys. Before he could think twice about it, his indignation boiled over.

117

"Stop it!" he snapped. "Let her work, or I'll go get the guard." Something in his voice knocked Tahar and Azouz off balance. It startled Hedi as well—he wasn't one to boss other people. But it worked. With sheepish grins, the boys backed off. They picked up their merchandise and started to leave the theater area, scuffing their sneakers to show they were in no hurry.

"Okay, okay," Azouz tossed back. "Don't get mad at us, Hedi. Oh, *please* don't get mad. You scare us."

When they had gone, the artist looked at Hedi uncertainly. "*Merci*," she murmured, and got back to work.

Unsure what to do next, Hedi stood awkwardly for a moment. Then he said, "I'm sorry. I—we shouldn't have bothered you like that. Those two are idiots."

"An artist meets that sort of thing," she said without turning.

Hedi watched for a few more minutes as she sketched a scene of columns and semicircular rows of seats with her brush. Getting up his courage, he thought of something else to say. "Do you paint for fun? I mean, like a hobby?"

"Well . . . I like it, obviously," said the artist, "but it isn't just for fun. I'm having a big show soon. I'll do two more paintings here at Dougga, and then at a couple of other Roman sites. It takes time. That's why I got upset when . . ." Her voice trailed off as she concentrated on the painting, and Hedi decided he'd better not bother her anymore.

The sun was dropping below an orchard of olive trees that bordered the ruins, making shadows of the stately columns creep across the stage. Already the air was chilly. Hedi gathered up his unsold hats, said good-bye, and trudged out of the theater and through the ancient streets, toward the road that would take him to his village about a kilometer away.

So the artist was coming back. It might be interesting to watch her work, a change at least. But what if those two pests came and bothered her again? Maybe she needed somebody to help her, to protect her from hassling, since it looked like her husband didn't want to stick around. The idea sparked a memory, something Hedi's older brother had said a week or so earlier.

Tawfiq had come home for a day to bring money for the family. At one point he and a friend, with Hedi tagging along, had gone to the village café. The friend wanted to know about Tawfiq's work as a waiter. Was he really making good money?

"You bet! But"—Tawfiq went on after pausing for a sip of his mint-flavored tea—"you earn it, believe me. On your feet all the time, running, and always with a smile on your face. It helps with the tips."

Then he chuckled. "Sometimes I do better by looking tough. There are all kinds of guys hanging around at these big resorts, and foreign women can get hassled. So some nights I wait around the lobby or the gardens, and if the manager sees something like that going on, he gives me the word and I just step in and put an end to it. I've gotten some fat tips, protecting the guests." He rubbed his fingers and thumb together lightly.

Now Hedi considered that word, *protecting*. Well . . . wasn't that what he'd done, in a way, when the boys were pestering the artist lady? Yes, that's what he could do, if she came back: he'd protect her. And she'd probably give him a nice tip, if he did a good job.

The next morning, therefore, as Hedi set out with his hats, the Roman ruins looked a little different to him. They might hold new possibilities . . . a new job, a step closer to the glamorous outside world.

The woman came at noon. Her husband, in a tweed jacket

and turtleneck shirt, again helped her get settled on the theater stage. Hedi watched from a spot where he could catch their words, thanks to the good acoustics of the ancient building, and heard the man ask if she wanted him to stay. Evidently reassured, he soon left, promising to return in three hours.

Then Hedi ambled over to her and was pleased to see a look of recognition on her face. "Are you working on the same painting?" he asked.

"No, a new one." She went on as though she welcomed his interest. "I'm doing the theater at different times of day, with different light and shadows, different angles. You can see so much change in just one place, you know, if you really look."

Hedi shrugged. A ruin was a ruin. How could it change?

He set down his stack of hats and said, diffidently, "I-I'm not too busy today, so I'll stay here to help you. I mean, if you need anything, you can just ask me. Or if anybody bothers you, I'll stop them. So you can work in peace."

She gave him a quizzical smile. "Well, thank you. I don't think I'll need anything, but . . . all right. Just so long as you let me concentrate."

But Hedi wasn't quite willing yet to withdraw. He was frankly curious about a man who would go off and leave his wife by herself. "Your husband . . . *monsieur* . . . he doesn't like to wait here?"

The woman pulled on her paint-smeared shirt, then shook her head. "He brings me from Tunis and then drives to a café in the nearest town and reads. He's a professor; he always has to read."

"It's nice that he lets you paint so much," Hedi said, probing a little deeper.

The artist focused on squeezing her paint tubes until the palette was neatly arranged with blobs of brilliant color. At last she spoke.

"It's an important show. My paintings bring very good prices now. I can get whatever . . . we ask. Yes, I suppose you're right. It is nice."

Settling down, Hedi watched as the woman sketched the scene, then precisely and delicately blocked in the colors. Soon he observed that she was painting both what she could see and things she *couldn't* see. There were statues taking form on her canvas, but no statues in the real theater. Nor were there any scarlet cushions left on the stone seats. And look at those ghostly Roman figures floating among the rows, some looking haughty and rich, some bending to chat with friends. Hedi watched, more and more intrigued. So that was what an artist could do—make the world look not just the way it really was, but the way she wished it to!

Now, what could Hedi do to help her? After a while he got up and hustled away to fetch a soda from a man who sold drinks at the entrance to the ruins. When he returned and offered the cold, wet bottle, the woman looked up in surprise.

"Oh . . . thank you, but . . . well, thank you. How much—"

"Nothing. It's just so you won't get thirsty."

She frowned slightly, then took a sip and placed the bottle at her feet. At that moment Hedi heard the babble of an approaching group. He stood up, ready. Sure enough, a large cluster of tourists were entering the theater. A guide spoke to them in loud French, but many soon spotted the artist and hurried over to watch her at work.

Hedi's cue. "*Pardon! S'il vous plaît!*" he said, trying for a firm voice. The visitors looked at him, annoyed and puzzled. He went on more boldly in French, "Please do not look. The artist must work hard, so please do not bother. She will have an important exhibition. You can see it later."

Disgruntled, they drifted back to their group. Hedi saw that the guide had interrupted his speech and was saying something about the artist. All faces, with expressions of high interest, turned toward her briefly, then back to the guide as he went on with his usual song and dance.

Hedi had done it—protected the artist! And something else, he realized. For once, he had *told* the foreigners, instead of beseeching and begging.

An hour or so later, Azouz and Tahar came swaggering into the theater. Caught off guard at seeing Hedi with the artist, they paused, which gave him a moment to steel his nerves. He gestured for them to retreat a little and, to his surprise, they did.

"What're you doing here?" said Tahar as Hedi followed them.

"It's a job," he muttered, thinking hard for a plausible explanation. "The theater's reserved for the artist today. I'm in charge."

Azouz sputtered. "*What?* I never heard of—"

"It's a new rule. Go find the tourists someplace else." Hedi turned his back on the other two, hoping his newfound bravado would carry it off, and a moment later he heard their footsteps shuffle away. He couldn't help a little grin.

The artist was starting to clean up when Hedi returned to his post near her. He studied the painting, in which the theater rose partially ruined and partially reconstructed, with figures drifting among the rows of seats and columns.

"That's really good!" he said.

"You like it?"

When Hedi nodded vigorously, the artist went on. "It's not done yet, of course, but—"

A man's voice broke in. "Finished? Let's see." The artist's husband was back, striding across the stage. Noticing Hedi, he said to the woman, "Is this kid bothering you?"

"No, no," she answered hastily. "No, in fact . . . not at all."

"I don't want any distractions, you know. You've got a lot to do between now and the show. Maybe I should stay with you next time."

"You don't really need to. You have your work—"

"We'll see. Now let's look at what you've done."

Hedi retreated to the spot where he'd left his six straw hats. He thought the painting was just fine and should certainly get the man's approval. But there was something about the way the man stood, leaning toward the easel, frowning, that bothered Hedi. It seemed as though he wasn't really looking with admiration or pleasure . . . rather more as though he were buying a horse.

Then the man placed the painting against the restored marble wall at the back of the stage, and started to fold the easel. "It's okay," he said. "They'll like it—it'll sell. Colors need to be a little brighter, but it'll sell quickly enough."

As the two left, Hedi slipped out the other side of the theater, jumping over fallen masonry. He hoped that if the artist came again, her husband would not stay with her. Not just because if the man were there Hedi wouldn't have his protector job, but because he thought the artist looked happy when she was by herself, painting away. She even hummed.

The artist returned alone the next day, midmorning. She did not look surprised to see Hedi waiting; she seemed almost to be expecting him. He wondered how much she would pay him. Or was "tip" the proper term? She and her husband obviously had plenty of money. He wondered whether he should bring the matter up. No, he'd better not say anything, not just yet.

"Many people would envy you," she said, "spending your time in this magnificent site. Do you like it?"

Hedi answered with a shrug. "It's a job. My mother makes the hats, so I sell them. It's okay, I guess. But I get bored. That's why I like to watch you paint."

"And what will you do when you're older?"

That was easier. "I want to get out of here. Go and work at a resort, make some money so I can have a better life. And so my mother won't have to work all the time." The woman was silent, watching him, and he felt impelled to go on. "I want to see the world, the real world like on TV."

"Yes." The woman had her paints and canvas ready for work by now, but she seemed to hesitate. "I suppose a person can feel locked up in almost any place," she said quietly, "even one of sheer beauty."

Hedi felt a daring impulse. "Why don't you paint a picture of *me* today? I'll sit good and still for you." It was just a joke, to make her smile. He didn't expect or even want her to paint him. He wanted only to share a little friendly joke for a moment.

But she turned and looked at him so intently he cringed with embarrassment. He'd annoyed her. Now she'd probably send him away.

When the woman spoke at last, her reply nearly floored Hedi. "All right, I think I will. Go over there and sit. Take the hats, too."

"Hey, I didn't really mean it! I was just—"

"Go and sit down. Any way you like, but don't move. And be quiet."

Meekly he settled himself below a row of columns. Now what had he gotten himself into? This was a fine way to protect! Suppose a big crowd came along—how could he possibly keep them from bothering her? Yet something in the woman's intensity kept him from speaking.

She stood instead of sitting, and soon Hedi noticed that she wasn't using her brushes, applying the paint carefully and precisely as before. Instead she was using a kind of knife, making broad motions with her arm. Frequently she backed away to look at the painting from a little distance, returning to it with quick steps. She seemed excited, humming louder.

Hedi's legs began to tingle, and he itched to move. She'd better pay him extra for this, he thought. But he kept still in spite of the discomfort. At long last the woman spoke to him.

"All right, you can come and see it."

He got up stiffly and went over to look, expecting another carefully designed view of theater seats and statues, with probably a figure like himself dressed as a Roman, sitting gracefully. But here was a mishmash of paint, and a big twisted figure that didn't look anything like him, just the green of his sweatshirt and pale blue of his jeans, and his dark hair all tousled—purple hair! And the columns—they made shadows on him that looked like prison bars! And the hats were skimming through the air like birds. This was a crazy painting, all right. *Crazy.*

"You're too close," the artist said.

He stepped back, then a few more steps, and squinted. He looked for a long time. And the longer he looked, the more it seemed to make sense to him. It was real, true, and in a way he couldn't quite understand, disturbing. Wild, like something struggling to break free.

The next moment he heard hurried, firm footsteps.

"I came a little early, Dalenda—" The man stopped short. "Dalenda, what's this? What on earth is *this*?"

She answered quietly. "I wanted to try something different today."

"Oh? Something different? I thought we agreed you'd do only

the Echoes series! Because they sell, Dalenda! Because people like them, they *sell*, you know. Who's going to want something like this?"

Suddenly words popped from Hedi's mouth, almost before he knew they were there. "I think it's good. I like it."

The man whirled on him and glared. "What? *You* like it, you little—"

From the corner of his eye Hedi saw the woman waver, then abruptly take the canvas from the easel. She approached Hedi and handed him the painting. Clumsy with surprise, he nearly dropped it, catching it just in time.

With a glance at her husband, the artist said, "Someone likes this painting. He shall have it."

"But—but, Dalenda! You can't mean it!" The air seemed to vibrate with his anger. Then the man gave a heavy sigh of exasperation and turned back to Hedi. "Well, kid, you've got an original Dalenda. Someone else would've paid a few thousand." As he turned back to the woman, his voice was flat and controlled once more. "I'll be in the car. Don't keep me waiting."

After the man left, Hedi folded the easel and did what he could to help the artist pack up her supplies. He held out the painting, but she shook her head.

"No, it's yours." She looked up at him from beneath the pink bonnet, with a hint of a smile. "And you're right," she said. "It is good."

With a brief thank you, the artist left, lugging all her gear. Hedi wanted to help, but again she waved him off. Watching her go, recalling the man's cold words, Hedi felt an unexpected anger start to churn inside him. And he knew it wasn't about money.

For a moment as he held the painting, he wondered what he

should do with it. Sell it somehow? A painting by this Dalenda artist would probably be worth quite a lot. But he dismissed the idea almost immediately. It wouldn't be right. Besides, the paint was a bit smudged where he'd juggled it.

His eye caught a gleam of something metallic on the ground, and he picked it up. It was the knife she'd been using—she must have dropped it in her hurry to get packed up. Again he looked at the smeared place on the painting. Maybe, he thought, he could fix it a little.

He set the canvas against a column on the marble wall and, holding the knife tentatively, tried to work the still-moist paint. Growing bolder, he gave the knife a dramatic flourish. Then, since no one was around to see, he stepped back, pretending to scrutinize the painting. After a moment he lunged forward to make another tiny dab. Aha . . . just so. Perfect! Hedi, the great painter! So this was what it felt like to be an artist, making the colors and shapes do what you want them to!

The woman would come tomorrow, Hedi thought, to look for her knife. Surely she would—she obviously liked working with it. And then maybe he'd ask her to tell him more. What kind of painting she liked most, for instance . . . and how a person could get started being an artist.

Carefully he set the painting in a corner where it would be safe until he was ready to go, then picked up his stack of hats. The afternoon lay before him . . . he'd better get busy and try to sell some.

7

Honor

A STORY FROM JORDAN

Y*asmine speaks . . .*

I was not exactly thrilled when the biology teacher teamed me up with Wafa Ar-Rahman. We'd be working in pairs, she said, when we started cutting things up—a learning experience I really did *not* look forward to one bit. And now I had to do it with Wafa. Not that she was obnoxious or stupid, but she was new in school, and so conservative and quiet and shy that she really sort of stuck out.

When I got home, I told my mother that my biology partner would be this girl Wafa, whom I could hardly even see, she was so covered up by her *hijab*. "She wears her head scarf over her eyebrows, and she doesn't say a thing. She'll be so *boring*, Mum," I moaned. "I'll hate that class."

But my mother was the wrong person to complain to. She was a hard-hitting investigative journalist, and she saw opportunities for social change and noble struggle in practically everything. She was so good at her job, in fact, that she'd won a special fellowship to study in London the previous year, and we'd all spent six glorious months there.

"My goodness," Mum said. "A girl from Beit es-Souf in the

glittering capital of the Royal Kingdom of Jordan! I don't wonder she's awed. How long has her family been here?"

"I think a couple of years," I said. "Her father's a manager in a food-processing company. Seems to me some of her country ways should've worn off by now." Beit es-Souf was notorious for its ultra-conservative, super-religious people, and for a girl like that to go to a progressive place like the Ayesha Modern School for Girls was *really* strange.

At that point I knew exactly what my mother would say next, down to the commas and semicolons. "You have no idea what her home life is like, dearie. She probably needs friends. You're very fortunate to have the chance to build bridges and gradually help her adapt, gain some self-confidence, independent thinking, and . . ."

I stopped listening. Both of my parents were very democratic. Mum just loved getting lathered up about social causes, and Baba's import-export business gave him a more or less worldly view of things. Justice, Freedom, Democracy! Equal rights for everybody! So I knew my duty. I would be civil and nice to Wafa, if it bored me half to death.

Wafa speaks . . .

I don't think Yasmine Fadlallah was very happy to be assigned to work with me in our science class. All the girls liked her . . . I think anyone would have been very glad to have her as a partner. But the teacher wanted us to work together, I don't know why. I resolved to be quiet and try my best, and not be a bother to her, even if we had to touch dead things.

Mama was waiting for me when I got home from school. She was always so eager to hear about what had happened at the start of a new term. I'd hardly had time to take off my coat and wet shoes—a slushy snow had fallen—before she started asking questions. It was my first term at this school, a very good school, which girls from good families attended, and it cost a lot more than my father liked paying. But he and Mama hadn't been pleased with the one I first went to after we moved to Amman, and he thought having a daughter at the Ayesha Modern School for Girls would help his reputation in the business world. I hoped they'd think it was worth the trouble and expense.

"Tell me about your classes, dear," said Mama as she poured me a cup of tea. "You're taking English *and* French? What is the science class like—what will you be doing there? Nothing that goes against the Koran, I hope, or Uncle Nabeel will be very unhappy."

We both laughed at that. Uncle Nabeel, who lived with us, had very simple ideas about the world, for an army officer, and he stuck to whatever the Koran said on almost any subject. If the Koran said the world was created in a thunderclap, then that's what happened. Not that the Koran could be wrong, of course! But it seems to me that you can sometimes combine different ways of thinking.

I told Mama about how we were supposed to work in pairs in biology class. "The teacher said my partner will be a girl named Yasmine. Her mother is a journalist and writes for two very important newspapers. Yasmine lived in London for a while and knows a lot."

Mama frowned a little. "Hmm. London. I hope she's still a good Muslim. I hope she doesn't give you ideas that . . ."

"That what?" I asked when she paused.

"That will distract you from your work. Don't let her talk too much. You're in school to study and pass your exams. Your father's not paying for you to socialize."

"Yes, Mama," I said, knowing she wasn't really as strict as that sounded. I knew she would have loved to go to secondary school herself when she was my age. But back then, there wasn't one in the village and her father didn't want her going to one that was about twenty kilometers away. Now she didn't do much except stay home, cook, and watch Egyptian films on television. That is, until Baba would come along and change the channel to football, or Uncle Nabeel would change it to somebody talking about religion.

Then Mama went to the kitchen. She liked to get as much of the dinner fixed as possible before Aunt Nihad got up from her nap and wanted to take over.

We were two families living in one small flat. Uncle Nabeel and his family had come more recently from Beit es-Souf. He had a new assignment as an officer in the Royal Army, a big step in his military career. They would be with us just for a while, Uncle Nabeel kept saying, until he could find a suitable flat for his family. Of course we all knew that wouldn't happen very soon, with housing so scarce in Amman.

My parents had one bedroom, my uncle and his wife had another, I shared the smallest room with my cousin Sawsan, and her brother Rasheed slept in the sitting room. I really liked Sawsan. She was nineteen, three years older than I, and very beautiful, witty and smart, like sugar and pepper. But no matter how much I admired her, it was only half as much as Uncle Nabeel did. He doted on her, as though she was one of God's angels.

Rasheed, on the other hand, was an oaf. He was seventeen and his father nagged him to study so he could pass his exams, but he wanted only to hang around with his friends. Rasheed had a big important assignment, though. Every morning he accompanied Sawsan to her job at an Islamic school for little children, and back home every afternoon. The school wasn't far, but Sawsan had to have Rasheed take her there and bring her back, to protect her. Rasheed hated it, but Uncle Nabeel required it.

Yasmine . . .

As things turned out, biology class wasn't really all that bad. The teacher had told us we would actually cut up some dead creatures, and she also kept telling us how very fortunate we were, because hardly any other private schools did dissection. Well, I never quite learned to love it—but Wafa, once she got used to poking around with a knife, first a couple of plants and then a worm, seemed to rather like it. Maybe it gave her a sense of power. She began to talk a bit and sometimes even smiled.

Wafa held one thing against me, however. I didn't veil. There were some others girls, too, who didn't, but we were a definite minority.

"Why don't you wear the *hijab,* Yasmine?" Wafa asked one day as we were leaving the classroom.

"Why should I?"

My mother and I felt very hot on this issue. Not long ago, she said quite often, most educated women wouldn't have dreamed of veiling, especially in towns. It was a sign of enlightenment not to wear the *hijab.* But today, especially with those radical Islamist groups trying to force their views on everybody, you really got stared at if you went bare-headed in public. Some people even said nasty things at you. It made Mum and her friends absolutely furious. Me, too.

Wafa's eyes widened at my snippy answer, but she soon came back at me. "Because religion requires it. If you're a good Muslim, you have to cover."

"Show me in the Koran where it says I have to cover all my

hair," I said. "Show me where the Koran—not some old male-chauvinist *shaykh*—says that women have to cover their hair. Let alone their faces! Yeeeh! If women have to cover themselves in order to be good Muslims, men should, too. They're uglier, anyway."

"But that's the point, Yasmine," said Wafa. "Women's hair is beautiful, so it should be seen only by their husbands, in order to avoid . . . well, you know. Disturbance. Besides, *hijab* is a sign to the world that you're a virtuous person, which is even more important."

"So every woman who puts a scarf on her head automatically becomes a virtuous person? I don't believe it. Like if you wear the *hijab,* you can be as mean and dishonest as you like and everybody will think you're good just because your hair is covered? *Really!* Being a good person comes from inside you, not outside. I would never wear the veil—my mother would kill me."

"You may change your mind someday, Yasmine," said Wafa gloomily. "You may have to."

That annoyed me, but I just shrugged. "All right, we'll see what happens. If wearing the veil is really important to you and helps you be the kind of person you want to be, then you should do it. But nobody should be forced to."

I knew that Wafa had no choice in the matter. In her village, in her family, the women undoubtedly all covered, and that was that. But I hoped the day would come when she could choose for herself—and that the day would *never* come when *I* had to change my mind!

Wafa . . .

I had sort of a serious talk with Yasmine one day about the *hijab.* It made me uneasy that she did not obey the rule of modesty. Maybe my mother was right when she thought that Yasmine might have learned to disrespect some things about Islam, living in London. I hoped that was not true. . . . I wanted her to be a good Muslim.

Then something strange happened just two days later. We were dissecting a frog in biology class. I'd been shocked at first—I'd never thought I would have to do such a thing! And the teacher said it was important because frogs look so much like the way *we* do inside—we *humans*! I'm not sure if religion would agree with that. Anyway we had to do it . . . and to tell the truth, I was getting a bit interested in learning about the insides of things.

The frog that Yasmine and I were given was a large one, and it seemed to be rather juicy, maybe too full of the formaldehyde to preserve it. I made a cut into the frog with the special knife—and it *squirted* at me! I mean, liquid spurted right out of it and dirtied my head scarf!

I squeaked in surprise, and everyone turned around and began to laugh. It was so embarrassing, just awful. Yasmine got a package of tissues from her bookpack and started mopping off my head scarf, but she couldn't do much.

"I can't wear it," I said, almost crying. "It smells terrible and it's disgusting. How can my *hijab* be a symbol of virtue if it's covered with stuff from inside a frog?"

"You have a point," Yasmine said. Then she got permission from the teacher to leave the room, and a minute later came back with a beautiful scarf—not the plain white fabric of my *hijab* but a finely woven, sky-blue wool scarf. I took off my *hijab*, and Yasmine managed to tie the wool scarf on my head so that it covered all of my hair. "You can wear it home," she said. "And you can keep it, if you want. I bought three of them on sale in London."

So Yasmine saved my modesty that day, even though she didn't agree with it. And strangely (though it was probably not the way religion would want me to think), I wanted to know more about

London—now that I had a sample of the nice things you could buy there!

Yasmine . . .

I told Wafa about how at first I'd felt totally confused in London, it was so different from home. It didn't take me long, though, to love the freedom and excitement, and that cool international school I went to. She kept asking questions, so I guess she was interested.

Then Wafa said, "I'm afraid I don't have anything as interesting to talk about. We're just from Beit es-Souf, and I never went anywhere else before. My parents sometimes still have a hard time understanding the way things are here." But at least, she said, they had relatives staying with them, to help them keep in touch with the hometown ways. I mean, I guess that was a good thing. I couldn't quite tell from the way Wafa said it.

"My uncle is an army officer and a very good one," she went on. "It's an honor that he has been assigned to Amman, in the palace guard."

"Does he believe in military rule at home?" I asked. It was not a very good joke, I admit.

Wafa frowned a little. "Military? No, not really. He loves to joke and laugh. When people come to see him, he makes everybody laugh. He says if you put people at their ease, they're more likely to do things the way you want them to. He says he hates to see long faces. Actually, he can be pretty funny, when he's happy." She looked up at me, with a quick smile.

"So," I said, "things are pretty much okay?"

"Yes, I think so," Wafa answered, slowly. "But Uncle Nabeel . . . he jokes a lot, but he does like to have his way. If something displeases him, he lets you know it! He'll be roaring with laughter one minute, and roaring with something else the next. My father tries not to disagree too much, especially as he—Baba—is the younger brother."

"What do you do when your uncle starts to roar?" I asked. Frankly, I couldn't imagine *my* father ever roaring. He and Mum always tried to debate in a civilized, rational way, no matter how much anger there might be underneath.

Wafa almost laughed. "We get Sawsan to deal with him. She knows how."

"Sawsan? Oh yes, your beautiful cousin."

"Yes. He loves her so much! She is his favorite thing in the whole world. That's why—oh, I shouldn't be telling you all this, it will bore you."

"No, not at all," I said quickly. "I like to learn about people. I might want to be a writer someday, like my mother."

"Well, all right," Wafa said. "Well, Uncle Nabeel is very happy these days because he has arranged an excellent marriage for Sawsan. To his cousin, who is one of the richest men in Beit es-Souf. In the whole tribe, really. He's older, of course, and he has a wife. But when he saw how beautiful Sawsan is now, he decided he would like to marry her. Uncle Nabeel and Aunt Nihad are very happy—"

Right then we heard, "Yasmine and Wafa, you are in science class, not a coffee!"

So we had to get back to work—and just when Wafa was getting interesting!

Wafa . . .

I loved sharing my room with Sawsan. Even though we kept bumping into each other and the bed was nowhere big enough for two people, we both laughed it off. She was like an older sister whom I could look up to, and she was so beautiful, with her gray eyes and dark lashes.

I didn't quite understand, however, about her forthcoming marriage. Her parents talked as though it was the most wonderful thing in the world, and my parents would look a little embarrassed and say they hoped that I would do as well, when my time came. But Sawsan would just sit there, and her face would close up, like a box.

One evening, as Sawsan and I were getting ready for bed, I said, "It seems your future husband is a very important man. You must be excited about your marriage."

Sawsan turned aside as she brushed her long, shiny hair. "Excited? Well . . . in a way."

I thought that over, then went on. "You'll live very well. He's rich, isn't he?"

"Oh yes. He has two large houses, of good stone. Of course, one of them already has a wife in it, but the one for me will be just as nice. It's brand new, I've seen it. And he has large flocks, and large fields of grain, and large bank accounts. In fact, he's pretty large himself."

"And," I said, trying to smile in a natural way, "you'll have a large wedding celebration?"

Sawsan yawned. "Certainly. Very, very large. I imagine half the sheep in those large flocks will be roasted. And I will soon get pretty large myself, I expect. And ugly. And then maybe he'll start looking. . . ."

She turned away from me again, but not before I could see that her mouth was quivering and her eyes were pressed tight shut. After a few minutes she said, "Do you have any more questions about my marriage, Wafa? Is there anything else you'd like me to share with you?"

"No," I said softly, knowing the coldness in her voice was not because of me. Then I said, "I'm sorry, Sawsan. I think you'll always be beautiful, no matter what, and I want you to be happy. Always."

"Thank you, Wafa." She turned out the overhead light and got into her side of the bed. Her last words, in the darkness, were just a murmur. "This is my fate."

We never spoke of it again. From then on, whenever the family was sitting together and the adults began talking and boasting about the forthcoming marriage, I tried to keep my face like Sawsan's, closed up tight.

Yasmine . . .

Something was wrong with Wafa. I could tell as soon as I entered the science room. She was sitting at our table, head down and shoulders hunched as though she wanted to shrink inside a shell, like a tortoise. I sat down and asked, "What's the matter, Wafa?"

"Nothing," she mumbled.

I fiddled around with my books and papers, then asked again. "Come on, Wafa. There is something."

"No. Nothing."

"Have I made you mad at me?"

"No! Stop asking. I can't tell you."

"Wafa, come on, at least just look at me. You're like a tortoise, all tucked into yourself."

Maybe it was the idea of the tortoise, which either insulted her or amused her—anyway, at last she looked up. And what a red, sad, puffy face that girl had! She must have been crying all night. "Wafa," I said quietly, "you need to talk about something."

Fortunately we'd both arrived at class early, and nobody paid any attention to us. Wafa hunched into her shell for a few moments more, and then she started to talk, so softly I had to strain to hear.

"We have a terrible problem at my house. It's awful, just awful! It will ruin us." She nearly burst into tears. Uncertainly, I tried to humor her a little.

"Oh, come on, Wafa. Nothing can be that bad, nothing can *ruin* you."

She glanced at me almost angrily. "That's what you think, Yasmine. That's what people like *you* think."

"Okay," I said. "Well, tell me, and I'll shut up."

With an audible swallow, Wafa began. "Yesterday when I came home, my mother and my aunt were shouting and crying like crazy, and Sawsan was there and they were shouting at her and hitting her, and hitting Rasheed, and I couldn't understand what was going on. No one would tell me. They pushed me into my room, but they kept Sawsan with them, shouting and crying and slapping. And I knew she had done something dreadful, something shameful!"

No sooner had Wafa gotten those words out than the class began and we had to be quiet. Wafa still looked like she would come apart with one little touch, and I was sizzling with curiosity. What could beautiful Sawsan possibly have done to make her mother and aunt so furious—and why were they hitting Rasheed, too?

Somehow Wafa and I managed to get through the hour without bursting, and fortunately we had snack time after science class. As soon as our school packs were ready, I steered her out of the room and out of the building, to a bench in a quiet corner in the recreation yard. She didn't resist.

"My mother forgot to make me a sandwich today," she mumbled. "And I didn't want to go into the kitchen because she and Aunt Nihad were there, crying and arguing all over again."

Anyway, I had plenty to share, because my mother always gave me big wholesome sandwiches with lots of vegetables and chicken, in the odd notion that it would make me lose interest in chocolate. After Wafa had eaten a big wholesome sandwich, she seemed to calm down a little. Maybe that was part of her trouble—she was just plain hungry.

"So," I said, trying not to sound too pushy, "go on. What had Sawsan done? And how did your mother and aunt know about it?"

Wafa started in as though every word had sharp edges that got stuck in her throat. "Aunt Nihad heard it from the neighbor . . . and the neighbor heard it from another neighbor . . . who heard it from her son. He'd actually seen them."

"Them? Sawsan and Rasheed?"

"No! Sawsan and a man! A young man, like a university student, and they were standing in the door of a café, talking. And smiling at each other, and laughing. And—and he was touching her hand! They knew each other—a man that we don't even know—that we've never even heard of! And she has been promised to my father's cousin!"

A jumble of scenes flashed through my head . . . the young couples in London, holding hands or with their arms around each other as they walked down the street, and sometimes even kissing right out in public, with lots of hugging and grabbing and messing up each other's hair. And nobody told them not to, nobody hardly even looked at them. Wow. I had to gather my thoughts before I spoke to Wafa.

"You're telling me that *somebody*—not even the neighbor, but the neighbor's neighbor—heard all this? From a kid? How do they know it was true? Maybe he was exaggerating, or misunderstood something."

"It was a boy older than Rasheed. He knew what he was seeing."

"Oh. Well, maybe he wanted to—to just cause trouble. Maybe because Sawsan wouldn't look at him, or something like that. I bet he just wanted to make a scandal. And besides, Wafa, everybody who repeats a rumor makes it worse."

Wafa moaned. "No, it's true. It's true, God help us. Sawsan admitted it."

"She admitted it? The smiling and laughing? And letting him touch her hand? Oh, that's shocking."

"Don't make fun of it, Yasmine! This is serious—it's terrible! My father's cousin will be so furious—oh, I can't bear to think of it."

By now the whole thing was starting to sink into my naïve little turnip of a head. Yes, if it really was the way Wafa described it, this could be very serious indeed for her cousin. I tried to speak calmly. "Did Sawsan say who this man was?"

With a woebegone shake of her head, Wafa muttered, "She would not tell. Only that he was a friend—and that she is guilty of nothing. But she is! We are disgraced and ruined, all of us."

Suddenly Wafa looked straight at me, almost fiercely. "You must not tell, Yasmine. Please, I beg of you! You must tell no one, no one at all!"

"But," I stammered, "there must be some way to handle this. The *shaykh* at your mosque could advise you, or maybe the school principal could tell you about some organization—"

She cut me off with a gesture, then turned away, her expression utterly bleak. "Oh, there is a way. It's the only way that will satisfy our people. You don't know about these things, Yasmine, but that's the way it is with our people. That's the way it is with tribal law."

"But this is Amman! You're not living way out in—"

Again she would not let me finish. "It doesn't matter! People don't drop their ways just because they move to the city, all those old beliefs they've clung to for years and years and years. They may even hold onto them even harder, so . . ." She paused, as though trying to figure it out.

"So—?"

"So they'll remember who they are. Remember what *makes* them who they are. What makes a man respected and honored, so he can hold his head up."

Wafa said all that in a tone of resignation, then stood abruptly and walked away, back to the building. She kept her head low, and I could see that she was wiping her eyes with one end of her head scarf. I didn't see her for the rest of the day.

I sat on the bench until almost all the girls had gone inside. I hated to think of what Wafa would walk into when she went home. I hated to think of what might lie ahead for Sawsan. At best, she might be quickly married off to that cousin, if he would still have her. But he would always hold this terrible crime against her—smiling at a guy and letting him touch her hand—and he would make her life miserable.

At worst . . . she would not live long.

The very thought made a shudder go through me, like ice down my back. How could these people think that way? It was so barbaric—so primitive!! No wonder Wafa wanted a shell to hide in.

Had I really promised her not to tell? I wasn't sure. The whole thing had sort of knocked my feet out from under me.

Wafa . . .

I hated to go home that day, the day I told Yasmine about the trouble my family faced. I had a good idea what to expect, and I was right. The men had both come home from work early, and everybody was in the sitting room, sunk in the heavy stuffed furniture and looking utterly hopeless. Sawsan was locked in the small storage room near the kitchen. That's where they had put her last night, and she could not come out except to use the bathroom, with her mother or aunt or me watching over her.

For a while after my arrival no one talked, just moaned and muttered. Then Aunt Nihad asked feebly, "Are you absolutely sure they already know in Beit es-Souf?"

"I tell you," growled Uncle Nabeel, gesturing fiercely, "they knew last night! Everybody in the whole village. I've told you that ten times. That man from Beit es-Souf, that junior officer from the Abuzayd family, he overheard me when you called, and he listened. He denied it, but I know he heard. He would've phoned his family the minute I left. Those Abuzayds, they're always trying to get something on us, they wouldn't miss this chance. My cousin called me last night. He wanted to know, was it true? I had to tell him yes. All of it. Oh, my God, my God! What has she brought upon us? Shame, shame, shame!"

Uncle Nabeel had been sitting up straight, but now he slumped back in his chair as though deflated. For a moment, even in his officer's uniform, he did not look so terrifying. Otherwise I would never have dared to speak.

"Uncle Nabeel," I said, just loud enough for him to notice. "Maybe it's not all true. How do we know? We just heard it from a neighbor who—"

"We heard enough! Anything is enough—anything is too much! She is from an honorable family, and she has been promised to my cousin, and we should have kept her strictly at home all this time. I wanted to keep her at home, where she would be safe."

He leaned forward and pointed his finger at his wife. "You remember? I knew the dangers here in the city, and I wanted to protect her. She needed protection—especially a girl that beautiful. . . . But you! You had to meet that woman at that school, who said they needed another teacher for the babies, and you wanted Sawsan to do it—she would bring a little money, you said. And *she* wanted to do it. She would have her way, that girl! She begged me, she begged me too much, the way she did when she was little, and I always had to give her what she wanted when she looked at me like that, and . . ."

He fell back in his chair again, and his large, stern face seemed to crumple, and we all looked away.

Then Aunt Nihad turned on Rasheed. "Rasheed! How could you! You knew what you were supposed to do, you knew how important it was. Why did you fail, you lazy boy? Why were you so careless?" She had probably already said this forty times, but there was nothing else she could say.

With a grunt, because he was too thick in the middle, Rasheed pushed himself to the edge of his chair. "Don't blame me—it was *her* fault! She knew how she was supposed to behave, and *she* failed. I never wanted to have to walk Sawsan to her job and walk her home, like a baby. You forced me to do that. I should be free to be with my friends after school. Nobody else has to look out for his sister, nobody! It's too embarrassing! And it's not fair. If you hadn't forced me to do this, nothing would've—"

"SHUT UP!" roared his father, and it was the only time I ever was glad to hear Uncle Nabeel raise his voice. I knew Rasheed's parents were very angry with him, and so were mine. But I also knew their anger would fade, because he was a boy, the only boy.

The room was full of silence for a few minutes, and then my

mother said, "Why can't we just keep her at home—not to go out for anything!—for a few months, maybe even a year. That is, until you find a flat of your own."

Uncle Nabeel shook his head. "No. It is not enough. It seems you still do not understand. My honor has been stained—dirtied!" His voice became louder and higher as he spoke. "My honor has been destroyed! What is a man without his honor? He is nothing, he is lower than a cockroach. He must have his honor, or he might as well die. *I must restore my honor!*" He thumped his knee with each of the last words.

My father had been quiet through most of this, as he generally was when a family argument started. The few times I had heard them disagree, my father tried to caution Uncle Nabeel not to talk too much about his views on social behavior and religion, that sort of thing, and especially in the army, among the officers close to the king. It would not do Uncle Nabeel any good to be thought a fanatic.

Now my father was ready to speak. "Yes, my brother, you are right. Honor is essential. But we are living in modern times. We're not living like a tribe in the desert, a hundred years ago. We have to make changes, adjust to the modern world. Your daughter has behaved badly, and she must be punished. But it is not worth taking her life. You can restore your honor in another way. Time will heal—"

"No, my brother!" Uncle Nabeel broke in. "You have been in this city too long—it has corrupted you. You're forgetting your values, the values of our family, our people. Some things must never change. This world is changing too fast for us, so we must hold on to those things tighter than ever. Above all we must have honor—and I must have *my* honor! I know what I must do, and you know, and that's all there is to it. Finish!"

148

At that point, even before my father could speak again, Mama stood up, grabbed my wrist, and pulled me to my feet. I know she didn't mean to hurt me, but the little crescent-marks left by her fingernails were still on my skin the next morning. "Go to your room, Wafa," she said in a flat voice. "You need to study."

I went to my room, my tiny room that now was too empty for me without Sawsan's smile and spirit. Mama shut the door behind me, and from then on I could not hear anything clearly, because they were speaking in whispers. Only once did I hear voices raised, and the first was Rasheed's.

"NO! No, I won't! You can't make me kill her! I won't!"

"Then you must find someone who will do it for us!" bellowed his father.

And one more angry shout from Rasheed—"All right! I will!"

Sawsan was doomed.

Yasmine . . .

When I got home from school, I found my mother hunched over her computer. Her hair, short and quite red because she'd used a new brand of henna, was unusually messy. I knew what that meant. She was thinking hard, massaging her brain with both hands to help her think, and grossly abusing her hairdo in the process. She was also smoking, which meant that she was so absorbed in her writing I'd better not bother her. Which was all right with me, because I needed to think by myself.

What should I do about Wafa's problem? Did it really concern me, or should I just mind my own business? In fact, it wasn't really Wafa's problem, it was her relatives'. And it seemed to me that the beautiful cousin Sawsan was kind of asking for trouble, being engaged but still flirting in public with another guy. She must have known it would get her in hot water.

But not such excruciatingly horrible hot water! I knew what might happen to Sawsan—"honor killings" were one of my mother's specialties as a hard-hitting journalist. And not only Sawsan would suffer. Wafa would be really messed up . . . Wafa who was so shy and insecure and who seemed to be just starting to come out of her tortoise-shell.

She'd told me not to say anything about it. But . . . maybe if I hadn't quite promised, I could . . . well, do what? Help Wafa deal with something too awful for her to face alone? Or would I completely destroy her trust in me?

So I pondered, as I sat on the edge of my bed, until there was a knock on my door. "Yasmine, darling," I heard, "I'm sorry I was so busy when you came in. Are you all right? Come out and give me a kiss and tell me about your day."

I got up and went out to the living room, where my mother was already collapsed on the divan, cigarette in hand. "Okay," I said, "but first put out that cigarette, please, Mum. It makes everything stink."

"My, my, what a sweet daughter," she said. But she put the thing out and then took a better look at me, and her motherly instincts shifted up a few gears. "You do seem a little subdued, Yasmine. Anything wrong?"

"No. I'm okay. Not one tiny bit subdued."

"Come on, child, sit down with me and tell me what you are, if not subdued."

"I can't, Mum. Please don't pressure me."

"Then I won't, dear. We'll just sit here and relax until we feel like human beings again."

That, I thought, must be one of her interviewing tricks. *You don't want to talk? Then don't. We'll just sit here.* The interviewees probably get so jumpy after a few minutes, they open up and spill their life history. And sure enough, before I knew it, I was telling my mother the whole awful story. And not least of all, my own dilemma.

My mother's face tightened up in anger as I talked, and she clenched one fist. And to complicate matters further, just then my father walked in, carrying three cups of tea on a tray. I hadn't even realized he was home, let alone puttering around in the kitchen. When I paused, Mum jumped up and nearly crashed into Baba.

"Hold it, girl!" he said, setting down the tray. "What's going on here? Yasmine, what have you been telling your mother, to get her so worked up?"

Mum was now pacing back and forth, fuming. "It's atrocious," she growled. "Simply *atrocious*. Here's the story, Hassan. Yasmine's classmate Wafa—remember, the one she carves up dead frogs with, the girl from that benighted place out in the desert—well, to put it simply, they have an 'honor' problem in the family. Wafa's cousin, who's engaged to some tribal bigwig, was foolish enough to let herself be caught in public chatting with another man. And now the girl's father's honor is destroyed, and he's got to do something about it, and the whole family is in hysterics."

"Oh God," said my father, sitting down heavily.

"Well, I'm going right to my computer and write an article about this ridiculous, horrible case and—"

"And use their names?" Baba said, now on the edge of his chair. "So everyone would know?"

She stopped pacing, lit a cigarette, and frowned. "Maybe yes, maybe no. We'll never make any progress fighting this idiotic mentality unless we can make it clear what 'honor killing' really is. Maybe I'll just describe the case vaguely and demand that the country move into the 21st century and outlaw these crimes and really punish anyone who murders—"

151

My father got up and faced her. "Hold on a minute, Muna. Think it through. I know you're upset, and Yasmine's worried for her friend. But we don't know all the facts—the whole accusation is just hearsay, so far as I can tell—and we have no idea yet how that family is going to deal with it. Don't get involved before things are clear—"

"And the girl is dead? Will that be soon enough?" My mother's words were so shrill and shocking, they stopped him short.

In the moment's silence, I got a word in. "But Baba . . . Mum . . . isn't there anything we can do? I mean, if Wafa's cousin really is in danger, how can we just sit around and not do *anything*?"

Neither of them answered, but at least they listened. Then my mother turned away from us, her face still scrunched with anger. "All right," she said, "I won't write anything. Not right now. But Yasmine is right, and as long as there's good reason to believe that girl's days are numbered, I'm not going to sit on my hands. There are other ways to intervene—and I'm not talking about the police!" She looked up at me. "Yasmine, can you find out where Wafa lives?"

"I told you what part of Amman, Mama," I said. "It's not where most of the girls at school live. The school bus really has to go out of its way."

"I need the exact address. Street, building, floor, flat number. And soon. Can you do it? Can you use a little investigative—"

"Prying?" my father broke in. "Meddling?"

"Yes, prying and meddling!" Mum answered, getting red in the face again as she glared at him. "Sometimes in this world you have to pry and meddle, or things will never change."

"My God," said my father. "You were wild enough before we went to London, Muna. Now you're worse—and you're putting a heavy load on our daughter."

She was, too. Truthfully, I thought they were both right: my mother to keep sticking her neck out for justice, Baba to urge caution—before you dive in and break your neck. But something clicked inside me just then, and it clicked on my mother's side.

"I'll do it, Mum, it'll be easy," I said. Actually I hadn't a clue how to do it.

Anyway, that seemed to settle things for the time being. Mum strode off to her writing room, closed the door, and got busy on her cell phone. Baba settled down to his newspaper and three cups of tea, and I went back to my room and tried to study world history. My mother was on the phone for a long time, and although I couldn't quite make out what she was saying, I knew she was talking to her friends in organizations that help women.

As things turned out, it *was* easy to get Wafa's address. Ridiculously easy. Wafa wasn't in school the next day, so I simply went to the school secretary and said I wanted to take Wafa some flowers and homework assignments because she was sick, but I wasn't sure of her address. The secretary said "God bless you" and gave me Wafa's exact location. I didn't even feel like a sneak, because I *would* have liked to take her some flowers.

Wafa . . .

It was hard to keep track of time, during those awful days. I wanted to go to school, because I liked school and I thought Yasmine would try to cheer me up a little. In fact, there was no one else I could talk to, and I felt utterly alone.

I wanted desperately to get out of that house of unhappiness. Rasheed was almost never home and even slept at his friends' homes. When he was around, his parents needled him and he shouted at them. My mother and my aunt now barely spoke to each other. My mother kept saying, "I want nothing bad to happen in my house! This is *my house,* and nothing bad can happen here!" My father, caught in the middle, would say, "This is *our* house. We are one family. We must stick together." Aunt Nihad sat staring into space, or at the TV, it didn't matter which. If she spoke at all, it was something like, "Never mind. . . . To me she is already dead." It gave me chills to hear her.

And Uncle Nabeel swung back and forth. One moment his face was so full of sadness I could barely even glance his way. Grief and despair radiated from him. The next moment he would be shouting. "What is a man, if he cannot control the women in his family? He loses all respect. I am drowning in shame—shame is all I have to my name now. I must win back my honor! And I must have proof that my honor is restored!"

Once when he was going on in this way, I heard my father answer him. "You may restore your honor—and lose out in your career. You know how the palace feels about this sort of thing."

It went on like this for at least two days. I wanted to escape, but I also wanted to stay at home, to guard Sawsan. Once in a while, if no one was near, I managed to speak to her through the crack at the bottom of the door of the storage room where she was locked up. She would assure me that she was all right, and then tell me to do as well in school as I possibly could, so I might have a future. Her voice was always full of tears and fear.

Then, maybe the fifth night after this calamity fell upon us, it happened. I had gone to bed but could not sleep. Very late, well after midnight, I heard knocking at the door of our flat. I opened my bedroom door a bit and saw my father go and ease open the front door, just a crack. Immediately two men, their faces covered by *keffiyas,* burst into the room, shoving my father aside roughly.

"The key!" one of them whispered in a coarse, heavy voice. "The room!"

Trembling and speechless, my father glanced at the table where we kept the key to Sawsan's little prison. The man saw, and grabbed the key. "The room!" he repeated.

He looked around, seeing two or three closed doors. My father seemed paralyzed. He just stood there, unable even to lift his hand, and the other man started to shake him.

Suddenly I had to do something—I couldn't help it. I couldn't think—I just had to do something—anything I could to protect Sawsan! I rushed out of my room and right to Sawsan's room, and flattened myself against the door, my arms spread wide.

"No!" I cried, choking and blubbering. "No! You can't!"

One of the men quickly pulled me away and pushed me, hard, down on the sofa. I couldn't resist, though I tried to kick him. I buried my face in a cushion, weeping. In an instant I knew they had the door open, and when I could force myself to look up, I saw them come out with Sawsan. She was limp, slung over the shoulder of one of the men. I caught the stench of tobacco as they passed me, and a whiff of something like the formaldehyde at school. It smelled like death.

My father, his eyes wide and mouth gaping, just stepped aside as they went out the door and vanished into the darkness of the hallway. I could hear their footsteps going down the stairs. In no more than five minutes, Sawsan was gone.

A moment later I heard Uncle Nabeel come from his bedroom. In a voice barely audible he asked, "Have they taken her?" I buried my face in the sofa cushion again—I couldn't bear to see the look on my father's face as he nodded Yes. A horrible, wrenching groan came from Uncle Nabeel as he returned to his room and closed the door. I heard sobbing from the bedroom for the rest of the night.

Yasmine . . .

After that shocking day when Wafa told me about Sawsan, we didn't see each other at all. She was absent the next day, when I got her address from the school secretary, and was out the next two or three days. I worried and worried about her, imagining what it must be like in her home.

In the meantime, I kept begging my mother to tell me something—anything at all—about Wafa's poor cousin. "Please, Mum, you *must* know something! You know, those organizations that are against honor crimes. I know you talked a lot to different people that afternoon when I told you—aren't they doing *anything*?"

She tried to be gentle and soothing, but as we sat together on the divan, I could see that she was just as upset as I was. "Yasmine, dear," she said, "I can't tell you. For one thing, these people have to work in public and in secret. They knock themselves out to educate the public and pressure the government, but if they're going to try to rescue someone, they can't very well announce it. I know they've managed several rescues, but I don't know just how. I gave them all the information about where Wafa lives, but I can't keep calling to ask what they're going to do about it."

I sat up straight. "Mum, remember what you told me about squeaking wheels? How a good journalist has to squeak good and loud?"

"Yes, absolutely. But sometimes a journalist has to know when to be patient. Relax, dear. Maybe you'll see Wafa tomorrow and she'll tell you that the family has found a way to handle the whole thing peacefully."

I knew she didn't mean it, she was just trying to calm me down. But I hadn't the will to argue. Maybe, too, she was trying to remind herself that there were still some people in this strange world who managed to solve their problems with reason and compassion.

The next day—I think it was the fifth day after Wafa told me the bad news, maybe the sixth—she was still absent from biology. I sat by our microscope and could hardly bear to read or listen or look at anything, my thoughts were so much at Wafa's crowded flat. After a while the teacher came over to me and said quietly, "Wafa has been withdrawn from school, Yasmine. You may work alone, if you wish, or I'll give you another partner."

I just shrugged.

After biology class, as I was heading for the recreation yard, hoping the bench in the corner would be empty so I could sit and brood, a girl tapped me on the arm. "The secretary sent me with a message for you, Yasmine," she said. "You're wanted in the principal's office."

I went back inside, unsure whether to hurry or drag my feet. But in the principal's office, my heart jumped. There was Wafa— and she smiled when she saw me! We kissed each other on the cheeks, the first time we'd ever greeted in that way.

"Oh, Yasmine!" she said. "Listen! The school called yesterday and said I had to come sign a paper or something like that, so I came, but there wasn't anything. Instead, the secretary had something for me—oh, Yasmine, I must show you!"

I didn't care what the secretary gave her—I was anxious to know about Wafa and Sawsan. "What's been happening?" I asked, grabbing her arm. "Are things all right at home now? Are you really going to another school?"

For just an instant a shadow crossed her face. "Yes, an Islamic one. But that's not what I needed to tell you, Yasmine. Oh, Yasmine—look!" She thrust a small envelope at me. "The secretary said someone had dropped it off for me, a nice woman. Look!"

I took out a piece of paper, folded several times to fit the envelope. I could almost feel my heart pounding as I read . . .

Dear Wafa,

First I must tell you that I am safe. You must not worry about me. Please tell my parents that I am all right, but I cannot see or communicate with them. I am staying with good people who are protecting me. I may have to leave Jordan and live in another country. I don't know, and I could not tell you if I did.

But I do know that you tried to protect me on that terrible night—that terrible night that saved my life—and I am very grateful, dear Wafa. The men were supposed to look bad—that's why they were so rough and brutal—oh, Wafa, I was so scared when they came at me, I was terrified! But they hadn't come to kill me—they had come to rescue me! And the plan worked—though I didn't understand anything till later, of course. Praise God for those good people!

But I weep so much for my parents. I hope they can forgive me—and that I can forgive them. I hope we can see each other again, someday. Please tell them all this.

With my love,
Sawsan

My eyes blurred as I looked at Wafa, and then I hugged her. I couldn't think of what to say, except the obvious—*Alhamdulillah,* Praise God.

Sawsan was safe, but gone from Wafa's life. And Wafa was gone from mine—Wafa, the little tortoise who looked so pretty in my blue wool scarf. . . . I would miss her—and always wonder about her, how her life was turning out. I hoped she would be happy enough—and that she would never have to be responsible for anyone's honor but her own. In my opinion, that is quite enough for anybody.

8
The Plan

A STORY FROM A PALESTINIAN
REFUGEE CAMP IN LEBANON

The moment the new art teacher walked into Rami's classroom, he and every other boy bounced up straight in their seats. With her cheerful smile and green eyes, her shiny brown hair and pink smock that said "You Gotta Have Art," she looked like all the flowers of springtime.

"We are very fortunate, boys," announced the principal in his best speech-making Arabic, "to have Miss Nuha Trabulsi to teach you art for the rest of the term. Of course, she has to go to other schools in the camp as well, and therefore she can come here only one day a week, on Thursday. But she will make you learn many things about art—how to draw and how to paint, and maybe other things." He glanced at Miss Trabulsi for confirmation.

She smiled. "Definitely," she said.

Rami thought, only one hour a week? And he'd have to share Miss Trabulsi with more than a thousand other boys?

Others might have been discouraged by such odds, but not Rami. After one good look at Miss Trabulsi, he decided on his life's mission—for the next three months, at least.

Actually, the whole thing was quite simple. Rami's handsome

brother, Marwan, was twenty-eight. All the female relatives in his family thought Marwan needed a wife. They fussed about it year in and year out. They schemed and plotted, argued and wailed. But nothing came of their efforts to marry off Marwan. Without a decent job, Marwan saw no point in even talking about it. Meanwhile, every day he was getting more beaten-down, more discouraged, more hopeless. He needed something good in his life. Like Miss Nuha Trabulsi, Rami thought. She'd be sure to cheer him up. All Rami had to do was find a way for Marwan and Miss Trabulsi to meet and to realize that they were meant for each other.

School suddenly became much more interesting for Rami. Looking forward to Thursday each week, he began to feel more kindly toward the drab concrete building, no matter how overcrowded and shabby it was. Like everything else in the camp. (The word *camp* always struck Rami as weird because it was no camp at all—nothing like what he heard the scouts did sometimes, up in the mountains. The camp he knew was just an ugly, makeshift, congested corner of the world for Palestinians to live in, because there was no other place for them.)

Anyway, here was something new in camp: art. Rami had never cared much about art, because all they'd ever done in art class before was copy cartoon characters, which got boring. With Miss Trabulsi, however, the boys woke up fast.

The first two Thursdays she taught Rami's class, Miss Trabulsi had them draw pictures with colored pencils. Not just the maps of Palestine and displays of gunfire that the boys usually liked to draw, but beautiful, imaginary scenes . . . blue underwater palaces, skiers in red jackets on brilliant mountains, clouds shaped like griffins, abstract patterns in rich colors.

"Because, boys," said Miss Trabulsi in her loud, clear, confident voice, "every one of you is unique. And every one of you has more imagination than you think."

On the third Thursday, Miss Trabulsi announced, "Good news, boys! I've been given some nice paints and plenty of paper. But now the bad news. No brushes."

A groan ran through the room.

"Oh, there's hope," Miss Trabulsi went on. "We still have a little money left, so if I can find any brushes in the market, we'll do some painting next week."

At that instant, golden-fisted inspiration struck Rami a swift blow and knocked him right out of his seat. He shot up, his hand waving frantically.

"Miss! I know where you can buy brushes! The very best—and at a good price."

"Oh, do you?" She didn't know his name. Not yet. "And where might I find these wonderful brushes?"

"I . . . I'll take you there. I promise."

Miss Trabulsi seemed amused. "Okay," she said, "let's meet here at ten tomorrow morning, since you don't have school."

Rami nodded vigorously. Then, suddenly embarrassed, he sat down and slid lower in his seat. His friend Mohammad made a quizzical face at him. *What's up?*

With a gesture to Mohammad—*Tell you later*—Rami got busy with his colored pencils. But pulling off the half-baked idea that had just popped into his head wouldn't be easy. He would definitely need Mohammad's help, in one way or another.

The minute school was over, Rami set out for the marketplace, the *souk*. He knew of two little grocery shops that sold some school supplies—poor quality stuff, mostly just pencils and dingy copybooks. But maybe one of them would have paintbrushes.

No, Rami soon found out, neither did.

He wandered up and down the long, narrow, muddy street, lined with tiny shops of every sort—the barber, plumbing supplies, baby clothes, groceries—and choked with stands full of color-ful fruits and vegetables. Here and there a pushcart heaped with once-frozen fish, trays of syrupy sweets, or stacks of red-clay pots blocked the way. Where was that stationery store Rami had heard about? He hadn't thought of going there earlier, because it sounded too expensive. "Stationer" was an intimidating word. Now, how-ever, it was his only chance.

At last he found the store in a narrow alley. Strengthening his resolve, Rami went in and confronted the elderly gentleman who owned the place.

"Please, I need paintbrushes."

Abu-Abdullah peered at Rami over the tops of his glasses. "This is a store for stationery, not hardware. We don't sell painting supplies."

"I mean brushes for artists. Please, you've got to have some!"

The old man hunched his shoulders and shook his head. "No, I don't sell things for art. You have to go into the city, to Sidon."

How could he go into Sidon? Even though it would be only ten minutes by car, he had hardly enough money for the ride. And in the city, no one would let a boy from the camp buy brushes on credit.

"Please, will you look?" he begged. "Maybe you have one or two brushes in your back room that you forgot about."

With a sigh of impatience, Abu-Abdullah shook his head again. But there was no other customer at the moment, so the old man began to frown in thought. Suddenly he lifted a finger, turned, made his way carefully among stacked-up boxes behind the coun-ter, and disappeared through a small door. All this time, Rami's heart was doing gymnastics inside his chest, flipping with hope, flopping with expected disappointment.

When the old man emerged several minutes later, he held a small narrow box. "I have only these. They were in a shipment of other merchandise that I got a long time ago. A very long time ago—on Noah's ark. I forgot about them . . . nobody paints much around here."

Sure enough, the box contained a dozen paintbrushes. They looked good to Rami. They looked worth their weight in gold. Abu-Abdullah mumbled a price that didn't sound too bad for brushes of gold.

"I'll take them," Rami said instantly. "All of them." And then he remembered that he had no money. He explained about his art class.

Abu-Abdullah's pale old eyes narrowed. "You want to buy all these brushes, and you haven't got any money?"

Rami nodded. "It's very important!" He braced himself as the old man considered the matter.

Then, abruptly, Abu-Abdullah said, "Take them. You pay later. I don't think I'm going to sell many paintbrushes the next few days."

"Oh, thank you, thank you! Here!" Rami yanked off his sweatshirt—his very favorite because, even though third-hand and made in China, it said CHICAGO BULLS. He dumped it on the cluttered counter. "You can keep this till I come with the money—it's a promise."

"Crazy boy, what do I want with your sweater? Here, take it back!"

Abu-Abdullah was still protesting as Rami rushed out. Success! And just wait till he told Mohammad how funny Abu-Abdullah looked, waving that sweatshirt around!

At home Rami hid the box of brushes in his room, as proud of it as a hen of her first egg. After supper, Marwan came home, wearily maneuvering his pushcart through the door. Heaped high with dishes, cutlery, boxes of nails, an infinite variety of useful goods, the large pushcart took up half the space in the cramped sitting room every night. But Marwan could not leave it in the alley outside the house, because although the neighbors could be trusted, who knew what strangers might be wandering around in a refugee camp of more than seventy thousand people?

As soon as Marwan had collapsed on the lumpy low sofa, Rami was beside him.

"I have something for you to sell, Marwan."

Marwan looked up, tired, baffled, and annoyed. "What are you talking about? I've got enough stock. *Everything for the House and Workshop*'—remember? I don't need anything else. Except half a million dollars to get us out of this hole."

"No, listen to me! You need these, my brother, you really do." Rami thrust a handful of brushes in Marwan's face. "Every home needs a paintbrush. And these are the very best. But don't worry, you won't even have to advertise—you'll sell them all, I promise you. And fast."

"You're crazy," said Marwan with a sigh. "Go tell Mama to fix me some food and then leave me alone. I sold a lot of stuff today . . . but standing twelve hours behind that rotten pushcart . . . is harder than climbing a mountain. . . ." A moment later he was asleep, sprawled on the sofa. Rami stuck a brush in Marwan's hand as a reminder, then went to find his mother.

The next morning Rami got up early. He had to supervise Marwan.

"You need a shave," he told his brother.

"Shave? I shaved two days ago. Who cares if I've got a clean face?"

"You need a shave." Rami pushed Marwan over to the small sink next to the kitchen. Quickly he uncapped the shaving cream, squeezed some onto his palm, and smeared it on Marwan's cheeks. "And you never know who may care," he said. "Now do it good."

Their mother watched from the kitchen doorway, enjoying the scene, even though she was as puzzled as Marwan. As soon as Rami saw the razor in action, he dashed to the tiny room he shared with his brother and pulled a clean shirt from the chest of drawers. When Marwan came back, Rami grabbed his brother's arm and started to thrust it into one sleeve.

"Kid, what's the matter with you? You're out of your head. Mama—" Marwan called, "Rami's gone crazy! First he makes me shave, then he makes me put on my best shirt. What's wrong with the one I've been wearing the last three days?"

"It's crummy," said Rami. "Put this on."

"Who's coming to the camp today—Madonna?"

"She might," said Rami. "You better be ready."

A little later he helped Marwan ease the pushcart out of the house. The box of brushes was safely tucked in between the screw-drivers and teapots. And Marwan looked pretty good. Rami had done what he could. Now, if Marwan would just do *his* part!

A few years earlier, when Marwan was a university student, Rami had heard him talk at political meetings in the camp. It had been glorious . . . Marwan up on a platform of packing boxes, thundering like a fiery angel! Words flashed from him like lightning bolts, flowed like spring torrents. He drove the crowd to shouts and tears with his passion and his brilliant language. Rami had worshiped him.

But that was history now. The scholarship money for refugees had been cut off, and Marwan had had to leave the university in Beirut. With no father in the house—not since that awful day when an Israeli plane went beyond buzzing the camp and dropped some explosives—it was now Marwan's job to support the family. But people living in the camp couldn't get jobs in Lebanon, and the best work Marwan could find was selling hardware from a push-cart. Rami, watching his brother grow listless and disheartened, knew that Marwan could not help thinking of the two years when he had been an engineering student, near the top of his class.

Well, thought Rami, things can change. He tidied himself up and dashed off to Mohammad's home. Mohammad, now Rami's partner in the plan, was ready, and the two boys found Miss Trabulsi waiting at the school gate. She wore ironed jeans, a green sweater, and a smile like a hillside of daisies.

"Good news, boys," she said. "I've heard about a stationer where I can find brushes. Let's go!"

Oh-oh. Rami would have to talk fast. "I don't think that man has any," he said.

"I'm sure he doesn't," echoed Mohammad.

"Well, we'll never know until we try, will we?" Miss Trabulsi started walking briskly, and the boys had to hustle along beside her.

When they reached Abu-Abdullah's shop, Rami quickly whispered to his friend. "Get her out of there before he can tell her about me." Then Mohammad went in with Miss Trabulsi, while Rami stayed outside, just around a corner.

A few minutes later, Miss Trabulsi came out. She was frowning. "Mohammad, why did you keep interrupting like that? That was very rude. The shopkeeper was trying to tell me something."

"Sorry, Miss," said Mohammad, "but you would never've gotten out of there if you'd let that old man start talking."

"Besides," Rami added hastily, "we know a better place, Miss. Honest."

After ten minutes of jostling through the crowds of morning shoppers, edging past carts overflowing with oranges and green almonds, carrots and tomatoes, Rami found his brother's pushcart. "Here!" he announced proudly.

"Here?" Miss Trabulsi looked over the spoons, extension cords, eggbeaters, hammers. "This is for housewares. I don't think this man sells art supplies."

"Oh yes, he sells everything," said Mohammad.

Marwan! thought Rami. *Say something!*

But Marwan, staring at Miss Trabulsi, was struck dumber than his pushcart. At last Miss Trabulsi looked up at Marwan, opened her mouth—and said nothing. She, too, seemed to have forgotten how to speak. What was the matter with them?

Rami grabbed the box of brushes from between the can-openers and teapots, and flourished them in Miss Trabulsi's face. "What about these?"

"Why—why—why—these look just fine," she stammered in a high, thin voice. "Yes, they'll do very nicely . . . if they're not too expensive. How—how much do you want for them?" She glanced back up at Marwan.

His face took on a deep blush. With an awkward shrug he mumbled, "Nothing."

Marwan, you can't do that! thought Rami. Why, if his foolish brother just gave those brushes away, then Rami could never pay the stationer for them—and Abu-Abdullah would go strutting all over camp in the CHICAGO BULLS sweatshirt. He would have to tell Miss Trabulsi how much they cost . . . and hope she wouldn't wonder how he knew.

"Oh!" she said, hearing Rami mutter the price. "Oh! Why, that seems very reasonable, yes, very. Oh, this is just fine. We'll have a good lesson in painting next week, boys." Miss Trabulsi seemed to have found her tongue.

She took a few bills from her purse and put them in Marwan's hand. Marwan did not even glance at the money. It could have been frogs, Rami thought, and Marwan wouldn't have noticed.

"Thank you," said Miss Trabulsi, and threw him a shy little smile as she left.

The two boys followed her, disappointed. Would this be it?

No. After a few steps, she stopped. "If that man has such good brushes," she said, "I wonder if he has any charcoal." She went back to the pushcart, Rami and Mohammad right on her heels.

"Ch-charcoal?" said Marwan. "Oh . . . oh yes. Not right now. I'll get some."

Miss Trabulsi smiled even more charmingly and left again. Before Rami could follow, Marwan grabbed him by the arm and muttered, "What's she going to do—cook shish kebab in class?"

"I'll find out." Rami gave his brother a reassuring look and hustled off to rejoin the others.

"Thanks a million for helping me find these brushes, boys," Miss Trabulsi said sweetly. She paused. "But I wonder how that man does any business, trying to give away his goods for free."

"Oh, he does tons of business!" Mohammad said.

"Because he's smart!" said Rami. "Everybody knows him. And he's very nice."

"Well, that's a good way to be," said Miss Trabulsi.

More than a week passed before Marwan and Rami could go into Sidon to look for charcoal. Rami had gotten a few more details from Miss Trabulsi. It was not the stuff you buy at any old grocery to broil your shish kebab, or even the higher-grade stuff for the "hubble-bubble" water pipe. It was a special kind of charcoal that

artists use for drawing. Marwan said the whole idea sounded ridiculous. But he had promised to get the art teacher some charcoal,
and he would do so.

In Sidon, Rami and Marwan traipsed along the main shopping street, asking in every shop that looked at all promising. At
last they found one that carried art supplies, including charcoal,
and they bought a couple of boxes.

"Crazy," muttered Marwan, eyeing one of the thin black sticks.
"Paying this much for a burnt twig. Well, if she wants it, she'll
have it."

Crazy or not, Rami thought, it was one more step toward his
goal. Now he had to engineer getting the charcoal into Miss Trabulsi's hands, and her money into Marwan's hands. Directly, if at
all possible.

Thursday morning, however, started with a dispute between
the two brothers. "You take the black stuff to your teacher," said
Marwan. "I—I'm going to be busy."

"What? You trust me to bring you back the money? You're
a fool. Get a friend to watch your cart and bring the charcoal to
school yourself."

"Come on, brother. I . . . can't. A little help, please."

What was the matter with Marwan? Surely he *must* want to
see Miss Trabulsi again, so why couldn't he use his head? Finally
Rami agreed to take the box of charcoal. Three minutes later, he
dashed off to school. The charcoal stayed right where it was, on the
small chest of drawers.

In art class they painted, fifty boys taking turns with twelve
brushes. But it was better than nothing, and with Miss Trabulsi's
coaching, imaginative compositions started to grow. When Rami
got his turn, Miss Trabulsi spoke to him quietly.

"Somebody left some nice charcoal at the school office this

morning, Rami. Do you think it could have been the—the paint-brush man?"

"Could be," he said. "Is it what you wanted?"

"Perfect. But how can I pay him?"

"Oh . . . well, maybe he'll be around somewhere. I'll see if I can find him."

"Thanks, Rami." Then Miss Trabulsi raised her strong, clear voice and spoke to the whole class. "Boys, next week we'll work with charcoal. We'll be doing something very different. You'll probably think it's pretty weird at first, but I guarantee it can make a difference in your lives."

Rami couldn't imagine how charcoal might make a difference in his life. Except in the one way he had in mind.

For the rest of the day he simmered in anticipation. Would his once-fiery, now-timid brother dare come to the school again? Or would Rami have to take the money to the paintbrush man him-self, thus demolishing a golden opportunity?

At the end of the school day, he hung around the art room. Mohammad tried to get him to come and play football in the street, but Rami said he was busy.

"Look," said Mohammad seriously, "I think you're just wast-ing your time. A lady like Miss Trabulsi, she can marry anybody she wants—a doctor, a big businessman, a politician. Be realistic. I mean, Marwan's a great guy, but—"

"Shut up," said Rami. In a refugee camp, dreams were hard to come by. He wasn't ready to give up this one.

When Miss Trabulsi finally came out of the classroom, he hopped into her path. "I'll see if I can help you find that paintbrush man, Miss."

The bright afternoon sun dazzled Rami's eyes for a moment as he and Miss Trabulsi left the shadows of the school building and stepped into the street. And then—yes! Across the street, in the shade of the one tree in the neighborhood, stood Marwan. He was wearing his good shirt, and he looked freshly shaved.

"Oh!" said Miss Trabulsi. "Is that the paintbrush man, over there? Let me put on my sunglasses, it's so bright." She fumbled with her shoulder bag, took out the sunglasses, and put them on. "Why, yes, I think it is the same man."

They met in the middle of the narrow dirt street, oblivious to a honking car. Miss Trabulsi smiled. Marwan smiled. Rami jumped around inside his skin. Then all three jumped out of the car's way.

"It was very kind of you to bring the charcoal to school," said Miss Trabulsi.

"No problem," said Marwan. Silence.

Marwan! thought Rami. *Say something else!*

"Well," said Miss Trabulsi, "how much do I owe you?"

This time Marwan was ready—Rami had seen to that. He told her the price he had paid, and Miss Trabulsi promptly gave him the money.

Silence.

Marwan! Do something! thought Rami, growing frantic.

But Marwan did nothing except stare at Miss Trabulsi, and she, so lively and bright in the classroom, seemed as chatty as a stick of charcoal.

At last she chirped, "Well, thank you so much. The boys are going to do something interesting next week. Rami, I'll see you. Bye-bye!" She smiled at both of them, and they watched her walk down the street, her brown hair shining in the sunlight.

That evening the two brothers were in their small room, Marwan lying on the bed in his undershirt, Rami trying to study. Their mother and their sister, Asma, a high school student, were occupied quietly in the sitting room. Suddenly the whole house started to rattle. It was Sitti, Rami's grandma, bursting in with earth-shattering news.

Cousin Muneer, she announced, was engaged to be married! All the negotiations between the two families had paid off. The bride's father had a thriving auto repair business, which Muneer could move right into, and the happy couple were warbling like canaries.

In their bedroom, with only a curtain for a door, Rami and Marwan couldn't help overhearing every word. Then, when the hubbub had died down, they heard Sitti heave a sigh that sounded as though it weighed as much as she did.

"Ah . . . Marwan. What a pity." She caught herself. "Where is that boy?"

"He's gone out with a friend," said Mama.

Rami froze. She didn't know. What should he do—yell that Marwan was right there, only six feet away from them? Too late— Sitti was barreling along like a taxi driver.

"Good, then. We've got to talk about that boy. What are we going to do? Every nice girl we've found for him, he says he's not interested. Stubborn donkey!"

"Poor boy, he's discouraged," said Mama.

In the bedroom, Marwan pulled himself up to sit on the edge of the bed. "God help me," he muttered, lowering his head into his hands.

Then Rami heard his sister Asma speak in exasperated tones. "He wants to choose a girl himself, Sitti. He's a modern man. Why can't you understand that?"

"Humph. He may be modern, but he's poor. Yeeehhh! I don't

know why we bother. He can't even think about marriage till he has enough for a decent place to live. It'll take a miracle. Too bad he can't choose a rich girl if he wants to be so choosy."

"Sitti," said Asma, "she doesn't have to be rich. She can just be smart and good and have a job, like every other modern woman."

"A job? Nonsense. A wife must stay at home and take care of her husband and children. All this business of married women going out—"

"This is today, Sitti! Girls don't want their husbands to support them right away. And what's more, their husbands *can't.* Marwan's not the only good guy who can't find a decent job—you know that."

Now Mama spoke. "My daughter is right, Sitti."

"It's still a shame, I tell you," said Sitti. "And anyway, how could he meet a nice girl, just standing·with a pushcart in the *souk* all day?"

"Nice girls go to the *souk,*" said Asma.

Her grandmother snorted. "People can't meet in the *souk.* It must be arranged by the family. That's all there is to it."

"Oh, Sitti! You're so old-fashioned," said Asma. A few minutes later Sitti left for her own tiny house next door, still quacking in disapproval.

All this while, Rami had not looked at Marwan. He could hear his brother fiddling with a string of worry beads and could imagine the look of misery on Marwan's face. He got up, went to the kitchen, and came back with a lukewarm bottle of pop.

"Here," he said. He put it on the floor next to Marwan and tried to get on with his homework. He hoped Miss Trabulsi was right about charcoal making a difference in people's lives. They all needed it.

Next Thursday, Miss Trabulsi came to class with her arms full of small branches . . . fig, almond, apple, pear, cherry. Some were still bare, others just starting to get blossoms or tiny green leaves. "You've no idea," she told the class, "how far I had to drive to find trees that weren't leafed out yet. Way, way up high in the mountains. Now, what are we going to do with these branches?"

She gave each boy a good-sized twig and then handed out paper and charcoal. But before she would let them start drawing, they had to look at their twigs. Just look, for a long time. The boys glanced at each other, grinning. This was *really* weird.

"Hold it straight up before you," said Miss Trabulsi. "See the pattern that the little twigs make, branching off the main stem. Now turn it a little, and see how the pattern changes. Now look at it from above, as if you were a bird. And from below, like a little ant crawling up the branch."

Rami thought it was pretty dumb at first. But as he studied his bumpy fig tree twig, he found himself getting more and more absorbed. New designs appeared with each change in perspective. He glanced around the room. The grins had faded. Each boy's eyes were now focused on the gray twig in his hand.

"Do you see how beautiful it is, boys, when you really look at it?" Miss Trabulsi said softly. "Do you see how many different ways there are to look at something as ordinary as a twig? That's the way with everything . . . there's always more than one way to look at it. Remember that. Now, choose the view you like best and start drawing."

That night, as he and Marwan got ready to sleep, Rami described what they had done in art. Tired and scruffy, Marwan was sitting listlessly on the edge of the bed. He peered up at Rami for a moment.

"She had you draw live twigs with dead ones? That beats everything."

"It does!" said Rami earnestly. "You have to look at your twig really hard, Marwan, and turn it different ways to see how it changes. Miss Trabulsi says that's true about everything in the world—you can look at it more than one way."

"Well," said Marwan with a heavy sigh, "there's only one way to look at me and my pushcart, and it'll never change. And I don't want to hear any more about your Miss Trabulsi!"

"I thought you liked her," said Rami in a small voice.

"Like her? Don't make me mad at you. What good would it do me to like her? A girl like that can marry a doctor. What would she want with a guy who pushes mouse traps and toilet scrubbers around on a cart? Especially a guy who can't even say two words to her. Leave me alone, I want to sleep."

Rami turned off the light and got into the other side of the bed. He'd felt so excited, telling Marwan about looking at the twig, and now everything was spoiled. Maybe his friend Mohammad was right after all.

But before he went to sleep, he had to get in the last word. "Just the same, Marwan, you better try it. Your pushcart's just a—a big twig."

A long moment passed. Then Marwan mumbled, "Shut up and sleep."

As the next two weeks slipped by, the weather got steadily hotter. The end of the school year was drawing near, and Rami had run out of ideas about his brother and his art teacher. He felt almost as discouraged as Marwan. His big plan was going nowhere fast.

One day, however, he came home with good news. "We're going to have an art exhibit," he announced to the family at supper. "It'll be part of the arts and crafts show next week. Miss Trabulsi's going to put up our best pictures in the yard of the community building, where everybody can see them. You've got to come."

"To see pictures of twigs from every possible angle," muttered Marwan. "I can't wait."

"You bet!" said Rami. Hope started to leaf out once more.

On the morning of the crafts show, Rami and Mohammad arrived at the community building bright and early to help Miss Trabulsi. With two or three other boys, they thumbtacked the pictures on a long display board. They worked busily—until Rami spilled the whole box of thumbtacks. He made sure they fell into a pail of dirty water that had been used to mop the courtyard tiles.

"Never mind!" he shouted before Miss Trabulsi could say anything about fishing them out. "I'll go get you a new box."

Miss Trabulsi called to him as he started to dash off. "You could look for that man with the housewares pushcart—"

"Good idea!" Rami called over his shoulder, and off he went.

Ten minutes later he was back—with Marwan, a box of thumbtacks in hand. Marwan's cheeks were a little dark, but he had on a clean shirt. Rami had seen to that.

"My goodness, what service!" said Miss Trabulsi, pushing back the baseball cap she wore in the hot sun. "But you didn't have to. . . ."

"No problem," said Marwan. "A pleasure."

"Well, thank you so much! What do I owe you?"

"Nothing. I'll just have a look at these pictures while I'm here." Marwan strolled around for a few minutes, then turned back to Miss Trabulsi. "This is good work, really nice. I . . . did some drafting when I was in engineering school, but nothing as pretty as these."

"Oh?" said Miss Trabulsi. "You studied engineering?"

Marwan nodded. "Beirut, a couple of years. Until the money dried up." He shifted his weight, cleared his throat, coughed slightly. "By the way, my little brother seems to be learning a lot in art class. He says you're really teaching them how to—to look at the world."

"Well, I'm trying to—" Miss Trabulsi stopped short. "Your little brother? Your—oh! Could that, by any chance, be . . . Rami?" She glanced at Rami, but he quickly got busy straightening one of the drawings on the board.

Then Miss Trabulsi said, "Ah. I think I see now. Rami is a big help and a good artist. And a *very* good brother."

Rami turned back in time to see Marwan smile. *Say something!* he thought, but he didn't really have to.

"Would you like me to bring you a cold drink?" asked Marwan.

"Oh, I'd love it!" said Miss Trabulsi.

"Or," said Marwan, "perhaps you'd like to come and, maybe, have a cake to go with it? Or something?"

Miss Trabulsi looked uncertain. "We aren't quite ready here—"

One more brilliant idea hit Rami. "Me and Mohammad, we'll finish this job."

Miss Trabulsi needed no more urging. Rami watched her set off for the *souk* with his brother. Marwan was talking. Miss Trabulsi, her face turned up to him, was listening as though every word were a twig of gold.

From any angle, it looked good to Rami.

NOTES

1. Santa Claus in Baghdad

It's hard to imagine a well-educated, middle-class family having to eat on the floor because they can't afford a table. Yet that's the way life has been, in recent years, for a great many people in Iraq.

Following the Gulf War of 1991, the United Nations, at the insistence of the United States, imposed heavy sanctions on Iraq, prohibiting the importation of an immense variety of materials and consumer goods. The stated intention was to prevent the government of Saddam Hussein from building up a war machine, and ultimately to hasten the downfall of his dictatorial regime. The most striking effect, however, was the impoverishment of a large majority of the ordinary people in that once-prosperous country. Goods needed for everyday life—pencils, aspirin, clothes, food—became extremely hard to get, and the problem was made far worse by the drastic drop in the value of money. As an Iraqi friend told me, around the year 2000, "You can buy anything in Iraq. It's just that nobody has any money."

Families sold whatever they could manage to get along without, in order to gain some money for daily needs. An outdoor market for second-hand consumer goods filled several streets in Baghdad. Given the choice between food with which to keep alive and a dining table with nothing on it, families such as Amal's chose to sell the table.

An especially critical problem was the lack of medicine and medical equipment. Many hospitals did not have the most basic medicines with which to treat the ever-increasing numbers of sick people, mostly children, suffering from malnutrition and other problems. Much disease was caused by contaminated water, because water and sewage treatment facilities were badly damaged during the Gulf War and could not be repaired. International health organizations estimated that over a million deaths could be attributed to this combination of crises.

Schools, too, were hard hit. Whereas education through university level had formerly been free to Iraqi citizens, eventually parents were required to pay from their very small incomes. Children went to school only a half day because the schools had to run in shifts. Books and basic supplies were scarce or nonexistent. The school that Amal is lucky enough to attend is better off than most, largely because many of the students are from families with government connections or some income from abroad or from business deals.

For years it was against U.S. law to violate the sanctions by taking goods and medicines into Iraq. Some organizations and individuals managed to do so, on a very small scale. The character of Uncle Omar in the story was inspired by one of my Iraqi friends, who made several trips to see family in Iraq, his suitcases bulging with all sorts of medical and nutritional items and supplies for everyday hygiene needs.

During this period, the 1990s and early 2000s, the sanctions seriously weakened the Iraqi people, without hastening any change in the government. In the spring of 2003, the U.S.-led war in Iraq brought down the regime of Saddam Hussein, only to be followed by a seemingly endless time of military occupation, destruction, severe civil disorder, and violence. How soon the people of Iraq will be able to enjoy a better life is, unfortunately, anybody's guess at this time.

2. Faces

One of the oldest continually inhabited cities on earth, Damascus is a fascinating place to visit. With a beautiful mosque dating from the seventh century, "Turkish baths" in medieval buildings, and a large covered bazaar full of goods and shoppers of every description, the old city calls to mind the *Arabian Nights*. Newer sections of the city boast wide boulevards, modern apartment houses, and luxurious hotels.

Against this exotic background we meet Suhayl and his emotionally trying life as the child of divorced parents. Divorce under Islamic law can be quite easy—for the husband. Family members, friends, and religious leaders often try to help save a marriage, for the family is considered a vital social institution in Islam and in Middle Eastern cultures generally. Nonetheless, a man who is determined to end his marriage can still do so with little trouble. Some Middle Eastern women's groups are working for comparable rights for wives.

Unlike the practice in most Western nations, in Islamic countries the father typically claims the children. They bear his name and are considered part of his family. Many people feel that a woman with children will have a harder time making a second marriage, because her new husband won't want responsibility for the children of another man. Although courts in some Middle Eastern countries are becoming more flexible in awarding custody to the mother, divorced women often suffer the cruel blow of losing their children.

Suhayl's growing awareness of himself and how he relates to others includes a closer connection with his Christian friend. Christians are a small minority in Syria. (In Lebanon, Christians are a much larger, wealthier, and more powerful group, around 35 percent of the population.) Generally speaking, the lives of Syrian and Lebanese Christians are much like those of their Muslim neighbors. While many Christians have pictures of Jesus and saints in their homes, however, Muslims would not have anything similar—even though they revere Jesus and earlier biblical prophets such as Abraham and Moses. Islam forbids representation of its founder, the prophet Muhammad, and other holy prophets, so a devout Muslim family would probably have pictures of holy places on their living room walls, such as the Ka'ba shrine in Mecca or the Dome of the Rock mosque in Jerusalem.

Some Syrian women have adopted "veiling" in recent years as an expression of their Muslim identity. The ones Suhayl notices in the marketplace have chosen an extreme form, which is rare. Covering the entire body and face is required in the radically fundamentalist society of Saudi Arabia, but elsewhere in the Arab world most women who veil simply cover their hair and wear modest clothing. Throughout much of the Middle East, except in traditional villages, most women and girls tend to dress very much as their Western counterparts do.

One inspiration for this story came from a visit I made to Damascus in 1999. The face of the long-time president of Syria, Hafez al Assad, appeared everywhere on huge posters in public places, a constant reminder of his power. Assad died in June 2000 and was succeeded by his son, Bashar; but the custom of plastering cities with the image of the national leader is not likely to disappear very soon, in Syria or elsewhere.

3. The Hand of Fatima

In the mountains of Lebanon, the soil and climate produce marvelous flowers. No wonder Sitt Zeina wants to build a garden to show off her roses! All sorts of fruits, too, thrive in Lebanon: oranges, cherries, plums, grapes, apples, figs. Lebanese food is among the world's most delicious.

It takes a long time to prepare, however, especially an elaborate meal for company. That's one reason why Sitt Zeina wants a maid. Another is that she's busy with several social, cultural, and charitable organizations. Many Lebanese women also have full-time jobs in the professions, business, and education; this is true, in fact, of educated women throughout the Arab world. And if they can afford it, they'll probably have some help in the home.

But where do those maids come from? No longer will young Lebanese women work as maids; they want better jobs. Most domestic workers these days are from Sri Lanka, the Philippines, or Africa, imported by agencies. But there are unfortunate consequences to this international labor migration, and foreign maids can be mistreated. Aneesi is lucky to have been hired by a good family, and they are lucky to have found a young woman who speaks their language—Arabic—and is part of the same basic culture.

But shouldn't Aneesi, a bright girl, be in school? Syrian law calls for education of both girls and boys for at least six years. Poverty, however, makes other demands. And as we have seen, Aneesi has dreams of her own.

Middle Eastern society, especially in less educated, more traditional areas, is still strongly patriarchal. While marriage arranged by families strikes most Americans as undesirable, the majority of marriages in the Middle East—as in much of the world—are still made in this way. Nevertheless, more and more girls insist on choosing their own husbands. Some urban young women decide to postpone or even avoid marriage altogether and concentrate on their careers, in spite of the high importance that Middle Eastern cultures place on marriage and family.

In any event, marriage does not mean an automatic "happily ever after" for an Arab woman, any more than it does in American society. That's why women like to acquire gold jewelry—and lots of it. In case of divorce, by law they can keep all their jewelry and similar personal possessions. The gold merchants with glittering displays in fashionable shops and exotic bazaars are selling a form of practical insurance.

Speaking of wealth, in our story, what about those amazing amounts of money that Maya leaves in her pockets? For many years, the Lebanese pound (lira) was worth about 33 cents, three pounds to one dollar. During the Lebanese war of 1975–1991, however, the value of the pound declined—until it was around two thousand to the dollar! At present the currency is stable: 1,500 pounds to the dollar. This means that prices are expressed in huge numbers—although actual prices of consumer goods are similar to those in most American cities.

The "Hand of Fatima" is a symbol used in jewelry and other decorative arts in many parts of the Islamic world. Usually a pendant in the shape of an attractively stylized hand, it conveys the idea of both protection and power. Charms intended to provide blessing, good luck, or protection are popular, such as blue beads and, among Christians, gold crosses and other images that can be pinned to a child's clothing.

4. The Olive Grove

I remember vividly my first glimpse of olive trees, from a train going through northern Italy. No matter how many I've seen since then—on the terraces of Mount Lebanon, the hills of Tunisia, the outskirts of Jerusalem—I still marvel at the curiously twisted shapes and the shimmering silvery leaves. No wonder people have cherished the olive tree since most ancient times, and that Noah's dove chose an olive twig, symbol of life and hope!

That's why the Israeli policy of bulldozing Palestinian olive groves is so horrifying to me. Whatever the official explanations, the underlying motive appears to be similar to the nineteenth-century American strategy of wiping out the buffalo herds on which the Plains Indians depended. Destroying a resource that gives people both sustenance and spiritual strength is an efficient way to break the will to survive.

The problem intensified after 1967, when Israel occupied the West Bank and Gaza, the last remaining parts of Arab Palestine. Instead of withdrawing, as required by international law, Israel established many settlements of armed Israeli citizens on Palestinian land, building highways to connect them. Even during the so-called peace process in the 1990s, the Palestinians increasingly saw their orchards bulldozed and their homes destroyed to make way for these settlements and highways. Palestinian towns and villages could be isolated at any time by military checkpoints, and people prevented from going to work, school, market, hospitals. These conditions helped ignite the popular uprising that started in September 2000.

Although Palestinians are Muslim and Christian, the conflict between them and the Jewish state is emphatically not an "age-old" religious battle. It is a contemporary political one. In this story, Mujahhid fights against Israeli *soldiers,* an occupying army; he's not fighting against Jews as people.

Religious identification does influence Mujahhid's behavior, however, as he believes his resistance is the sort of jihad called for by Islam. In the West, the term *jihad* is often translated as "holy war," suggesting an incorrect image of Muslims spreading their faith by the sword. The real meaning is "struggle, striving." Since this can include fighting to defend religion and oppose aggression, the idea can, unfortunately, be used for extremist purposes. A more basic interpretation of *jihad* refers to inner struggle: each person's effort to overcome moral weakness and to strive for justice. Throughout much of its history Islam has been a remarkably tolerant religion— and perhaps Mujahhid's own religious understanding grows a little broader by the end of his story.

5. In Line

What is a city family like Rania's doing in a village? In Egypt many government employees are sent to rural areas to carry out social, technical, and agricultural programs. Salaries are low and living conditions quite different from the city—even though, with Egypt's large and growing population, a "village" is often a good-sized town. Understandably, city people may find it difficult to adjust to the new way of life, which can promote feelings of class-consciousness.

That's one reason why Rania's mother decides to wear her head-covering when Fayza comes to the house. In the past thirty years or so, many urban women and girls in Egypt have adopted the Islamic practice of "veiling," which earlier had been rejected by most educated Egyptian women. There are several explanations for this trend: religious, social, political, even "fashion." Mrs. Gamal's reasons may be religious; but in this case she seems to be emphasizing her difference from the village women, who typically wear just a small, colorful scarf as part of their traditional dress.

In social matters, Egypt is a fairly conservative country. Young boys and girls go to school together, but at about the age of twelve are usually separated and sent to single-sex schools. Some progressive private schools in the city do have co-education, as do some villages that cannot afford separate schools for girls and boys. Because of Egypt's dense population and economic difficulties, public schooling leaves a lot to be desired. Many students in the public schools go for shortened school days, and although universal education is required in principle, some poor children don't go at all. Families who can pay for it usually send their children to private schools; but even among private schools, the quality varies a great deal.

Exams are all-important, starting in first grade, and teachers focus their lessons strictly on preparing students for the exams. At the end of secondary school, students must take a battery of difficult exams. Because teachers are very poorly paid, they supplement their income by private tutoring; and because most students can't get adequately prepared in school, they must supplement their regular schooling by being tutored. It's a troublesome and unfair situation, as many families can't afford the extra help.

An Egyptian middle-class girl with progressive parents can aim at a wide range of professional careers. The educational system, however, steers university students into different professions according to their results on the secondary school exams. For instance, a girl who passes the exams with high marks usually goes into medical studies—even though she might prefer to study art or literature. In rural areas, a girl like Fayza can also aspire to a white-collar profession, but it will take a lot of determination on her part and strong support from her parents.

Egyptians are famous for their good humor and their love of laughing. It shines through in spite of the difficulties they face every day in a politically and economically stressed society. Even poor people will be generous toward a visitor, sharing whatever they have in the way of food and hospitality. And Egypt does have lovely flowers, plentiful and inexpensive. The roses bloom all winter—although they do tend to droop too soon!

6. Scenes in a Roman Theater

Many artists find the luminous skies of North Africa an inspiration for their work. Groves of twisted old olive trees, carpets of wild flowers blooming during the cool winter season, palm-filled desert oases and the sparkling waters of the Mediterranean, picturesque whitewashed farm houses—Tunisia offers the artist endless possibilities! Like Dalenda in this story, I once spent many pleasant hours painting scenes of Tunisia for a show . . . and like Dalenda, I sometimes got hassled by the local kids.

Besides the beauties of nature, Tunisia's magnificent heritage from antiquity is spectacular. The country flourished during a long period of Roman rule (roughly from the first century BC to the fifth century AD), and the Romans left impressive reminders of their civilization, such as immense public baths, circuses for gladiatorial "games" and execution of Christian martyrs, awe-inspiring aqueducts, temples, and in a few places, whole towns. Some sites, such as the one in this story, Dougga, never had later constructions built upon them and therefore give us a good idea of what an ancient town was like.

In modern times, after gaining independence from French colonial rule in 1956, Tunisia appeared to be a model state among the Arab nations of North Africa and the Middle East. A progressive government brought its people important reforms, especially regarding women's rights. Today, however, under an authoritarian regime, life is less free.

Tunisia is still a dream place to visit, especially for Europeans from countries with cold, gray skies. But tourism is a double-faced blessing. In Tunisia large, gaudy hotels have sprung up along the coast with its many miles of beautiful beaches, and young people are lured by the promise of money that can be earned at resorts. While tourism brings much-needed income, it also encourages tastes and attitudes that may undermine the traditional culture and values. It's the same story all over the Mediterranean, all over the "holiday" world. Perhaps Hedi, "the great artist," will someday help to keep Tunisian culture alive.

7. Honor

Just what is "honor killing"? Usually a crime described in this way occurs when a woman or girl, in her family's eyes, steps over the line of proper behavior regarding the opposite sex. If she is married, this could mean infidelity to her husband. If she is not married, perhaps she has been sexually active, or has a boyfriend and sees him without her family's approval, or refuses to marry the man her family has chosen for her. In extreme cases, a girl or woman can be accused of "immoral behavior" if she simply speaks to a man in public, or if she has been raped, or even if she just sits next to a man on the bus!

If something like this happens, the whole family is affected—especially the woman's father. Claiming that his personal honor has been violated, he feels deeply shamed and disgraced. The family may decide that the only way to remove the stain on his honor is with the blood of the allegedly guilty young woman. They may claim that the murder was hardly a crime at all—rather, a "necessity" to restore the father's and the family's honor. Sometimes a brother in his middle teens is told to carry out the family's decision to kill his sister, because if the case comes to court, the boy will be judged more leniently than an adult would be.

The sources for the tradition of "honor killing" are ancient and lie mainly in tribal culture. Middle Eastern tribal society is heavily patriarchal, which means that the father is responsible for the welfare of everyone in his household, especially the women, and has complete authority and power over them. If any of the women act against his wishes, therefore, it appears that he is unable to control their behavior. He appears weak, and his standing in the tribe or community is undermined.

It must be emphasized, however, that "honor crime" is not something particular to Arab society. It is also a serious problem in such countries as Turkey and Pakistan. Nor is this type of killing based on religion. The beliefs of Islam do not accept it—indeed, the teachings of the prophet Mohammad call for fair and compassionate treatment of women. Although actual murder of women for allegedly "immoral behavior" is not a problem in southern European societies such as Greece and Italy, the concepts of honor and shame are extremely important values throughout much of the Mediterranean world, in both Muslim and Christian populations.

In recent years, some countries have seen what appears to be a resurgence of "honor crime," possibly because the problem has come more into the open and is increasingly recognized as a public concern, rather than a private matter for families to deal with. The unsettling effects of social change may also have a lot to do with it, such as migration from rural villages into the alien world of big cities. Under stress, people often want to hold on to the "old ways," especially male dominance, in an attempt to maintain social control and as a form of psychological reassurance.

Since the 1990s, a small but growing number of people in the Arab world have been trying to combat the problem of "honor crime." Jordan, where an average of twenty-five "honor crimes" are reported every year, has been especially active in this effort, through organized campaigns, media publicity, safe houses where threatened women can be protected, and public demonstrations. Social activists have tried repeatedly to persuade the Jordanian Parliament to tighten criminal laws and impose much more severe punishment on persons found guilty of "honor crimes." This is essential, because as long as the actual murderer gets only a very light sentence or even goes free, some people will continue to commit crimes against women simply by pleading that they acted "in a fit of fury."

Although the problem may be decreasing in Jordan, resistance to change is still strong. The tribal mindset with its assumptions about women's responsibility for men's honor is still entrenched in parts of Arab society. It will probably take many more years of legal work and public education before this social scourge is overcome.

8. The Plan

Rami the dreamer tries hard to keep his hopes high. And that's a good thing, because there's not much else going for him.

As a Palestinian growing up in a refugee camp, he is a tiny part of the longest-lasting, largest, and most difficult refugee problem in the world. Possibly a few million Palestinians (it's hard to come up with accurate numbers) live outside what they consider their homeland of Palestine, most of them against their will. The problem goes back to 1948 when, with the creation of the new Jewish state of Israel in what had been the Arab state of Palestine, around 750,000 Palestinians were forced to leave their homes. Some had the means to settle down elsewhere and start new lives, but the great majority had no choice but to seek refuge in the neighboring Arab states.

At first they lived in makeshift tents provided by the United Nations—which probably led to calling the refugee communities "camps." When it became clear that the refugees would not be allowed to return to their homes, those tents were replaced by makeshift, cinderblock buildings. Generations of Palestinians have been living in these camps ever since, in poverty and bleak, badly overcrowded conditions.

Some people argue that just as Israel took in Jews from all over the world, the Arab states should have "taken in" the Palestinians. But Israel was founded for the express purpose of being a home for any and all Jews, whereas the Arab states saw no reason why they should have to incorporate an additional—and very unhappy—population. (Keep in mind that although the Arab lands are huge, most of that territory is desert and cannot support large numbers of people.) Even more important, the Palestinians do not want to settle down permanently in other Arab states. They want to live in their own homeland: Palestine.

The situation in Lebanon is particularly difficult. More than 400,000 Palestinians now live in that very small country, about half of them in twelve official camps. Because of the combination of religious groups in Lebanon, the Lebanese government is afraid that the addition of all those Palestinians would upset the complicated balance. Furthermore, the economy of Lebanon is weak and jobs are scarce. Palestinians must therefore find work in the camps, or only the most menial, poorly paid types of work outside them.

Since the nineteenth century, Palestinians have placed high value on education, which continues today. Numerous organizations, both Palestinian and international, try to help the refugees in Lebanon and elsewhere. The United Nations, through the UN Relief and Works Agency (UNRWA), has provided schools and scholarships since the start of the refugee problem, although the schools are badly overcrowded and funding is frequently cut back. It was my visit to an UNRWA school a few years ago, in fact, that gave me the idea for a story about "Rami," with his spirit and determination.

Some non-governmental groups teach women to do the beautiful embroidery for which Palestinian culture is renowned, and earn a little income from selling it. Other organizations work with children on creative projects—art, writing, film-making, collection of oral history, music and traditional folkdance—to help preserve and demonstrate pride in Palestinian culture.

But these efforts don't reach everyone—and an educated person has little chance of finding satisfying work. Rami's brother, Marwan, is already stuck in that trap. If the situation of the Palestinians continues as it is, many of Rami's classmates may lose all hope for the future and turn to extremist groups. This prospect is not the least of the many critical reasons for Israel and the Palestinians to reach a resolution based on justice and security for all—and for the United States to help in the most effective way possible.

Much of the action in this story takes place in the *souk*—the traditional market area, full of shops and vendors. A common sight in the *souk* is a café where men sit smoking the *narghileh*.

ELSA MARSTON

grew up in Newton, Massachusetts. She was educated at Vassar College; University of Iowa; Harvard University, where she earned her Masters in International Affairs; and Indiana University, where she received an M.S. in Art Education. A Rotary Fellowship enabled her to pursue her interest in the Middle East; she attended the American University of Beirut, Lebanon, where she met her husband, the late Iliya Harik, Professor Emeritus of Political Science at Indiana University. Marston is the author of many works of fiction and nonfiction, including *Women in the Middle East: Tradition and Change; The Ugly Goddess; Muhammad of Mecca, Prophet of Islam; The Ancient Egyptians;* and *A Griffin in the Garden.* She has three grown sons and lives in Bloomington, Indiana.